FIC
BER

Berry, Ber

Redemption song.

$21.95

DATE		

redemption song

Also by Bertice Berry

I'm on My Way But Your Foot Is on My Head:
A Black Woman's Story of
Getting Over Life's Hurdles

Sckraight from the Ghetto:
You Know You're Ghetto If . . .

You Still Ghetto:
You Know You're Still Ghetto If . . .

redemption song

a novel

doubleday

new york london toronto sydney auckland

bertice berry

PUBLISHED BY DOUBLEDAY
a division of Random House, Inc.
1540 Broadway, New York, New York 10036

DOUBLEDAY and the portrayal of an anchor with a dolphin
are trademarks of Doubleday, a division of Random House, Inc.

Book design by Donna Sinisgalli.

Library of Congress Cataloging-in-Publication Data
Berry, Bertice
Redemption song/Bertice Berry.— 1st ed.
p. cm.
1. Afro-Americans—Fiction. I. Title.
PS3552.E7425 R43 2000
813′.54—dc21
99-055781

ISBN 0-385-49844-6

For Emma Rogers, Atlanta Brown, Karen Denton,
and all the booksellers, librarians, and teachers
who encourage us to read

If you ask black people whether or not they believe in reincarnation, most of them will tell you they don't. But these same people will look at a baby and say, "That child's been here before." Black folks see reincarnation as a way of working out the unfulfilled longings of their ancestors.

—Cosina Brown

prologue

🔥 Our love was sweet and tart like lemonade on a sun-scorched day or the sweat that runs down your lover's face. It was bittersweet, more bitter than sweet. But by the time you find this, you gonna get to the sweet, cause me and Joe done worked out all the bitter.

This is my story, mine and yours, my children of grace....

I'm writing these words so everybody can know that God be real. Spirit be real. Love be real.

I don't know how I come to do it. But I am. I never learn to write or read. But here I be doing it. All I know is I got to do it fast, cause my life here ain't gonna be long. I gotta do what I'm sposed to. I guess this been the reason all along. I never knowed why a person has to go through so much pain, just to get to the comfort. But I reckon comfort only comes to those who suffer.

I better write now, fore this power leave me.

Cosina Brown, or Miss Cozy, as she was known throughout the literary community, relaxed herself into her favorite chair and smiled. "Hello, old friend," she said to the book, *Children of Grace*, she held in her lap. Even though she loved books passionately—she sold them for a living—this book was special.

"Been a long time since I read you. Something's telling me to read you again, and you know I *always* listen to the 'something's.'

"Sweet Honey got a song about that. It says listen more often to *things* than to beings, because in them we hear the ancestors prayers."

Miss Cozy shifted herself in the overstuffed chair, and got more comfortable. Reading this book always brought on change. A major shift was coming, Miss Cozy could feel it, so she knew she had to get ready. As she began to reread *Children of Grace,* the only known copy of a slave woman's journal, the words seemed to leap off the pages and connect with her thoughts. Somewhere, in the middle of reading, Miss Cozy could tell that she was not reading at all. She was asleep, but someone or something was reading the book to her.

I don't know when I was borned, but now I know why. I was put here to tell a story. A story of love. Cause love is powerful and can't nothing stop it. Not even the place I'm in can stop my love. They call it slavery. I call it death.

I was saying that I don't know where I was borned. Don't know my real people neither. Just the man who raise me. I ain't find out til I was on in my life that he wasn't my daddy.

We were sold to the same plantation on the same day. My blood mama was killed trying to run. Old man Hunn wasn't so old then. He was out hunting my mama and me. He wasn't a real catcher. Others caught slaves for money. He caught em for keeps.

Anyway, Hunn catch up with my mama and me, cause she need to stop and feed me.

Story go that he laid eyes on her and he just knowed that he had his best find ever.

But my mama wouldn't be caught easy. She was pure-blood African, and full of fire.

He catch her unawares, snatch me from her breast, and they say, he try to get that milk for hisself. Now I was way too young to remember, but that's the story I hear.

That there is a sickness, pure and simple. But anybody trying to keep folks like animals got to be sick.

My mama was caught by surprise, but she had one for him, too.

In her pocket she have a sharp piece of something that she make and slice him right cross his eyes.

Old man Hunn didn't have to think about what he was gonna do.

He hold up his gun and shoot her dead in the face.

Folks say she didn't die right away, but sometimes folks say things to make you feel a bit better after having to hear a bunch of pain. Wasn't nothing bout that story that made me feel any better. Anyway, that's about all I know bout my real mama. Sometimes I think I can still taste that sweet milk.

1.

You Make Me Feel Like Myself

Ross Buchanan was in front of Black Images bookstore at seven-thirty in the morning; he was on a mission. He knew the bookstore didn't open until eight o'clock but he wanted to be there when the owner, Cosina Brown, opened her doors. He'd been there before to pick up what he called a "popular culture book." As an anthropologist, he spent most of his time looking for artifacts or in university libraries digging around in the stacks. Modern books by modern writers were rarely on his agenda. Miss Cozy's bookstore sold its share of *New York Times* bestsellers, but Black Images also specialized in rare, hard-to-find books. Ross wasn't a regular like most of Miss Cozy's other customers, but today, Ross Buchanan sat on the bench in front of Black Images hoping for a miracle. While he waited, he unfolded the copy of an old letter he always carried with him.

Dear Iona,

> *I write to you, but I know you won't be gettin this. I be free for going on five years now. But I ain't truly free, cause I ain't with you. Mr. Sanders, the man who help me get free, say maybe I can buy you free, too. I'm a try. Cause what good is this freedom, if I ain't free to love you?*

> *I guess I'm just writin cause I can. Mr. Sanders, he teach me that, too. I'm a write again tomorrow, maybe them stars you be talkin to will tell you what this say.*

> *I love you, you make me feel like myself.*

> *Joe*

Ross refolded the worn copy of the old letter and closed his eyes and said a prayer: "Please God, let Miss Cozy know something about *Children of Grace*. Amen."

2.

Seek Peace, Find Love

Ross Buchanan had finally taken a sabbatical from teaching anthropology after ten long years. He was one of the best professors at one of the best universities, but he needed to be much more than that. While he was working on his Ph.D., he'd heard about an enslaved man named Joe who'd written letters to a woman he was sold away from. The letters never reached her. It was said that all but the one he held had been destroyed. The woman Iona had also written about this love in a memory book called *Children of Grace*.

Finding that book was extremely important to Ross. Unfortunately, many of his colleagues didn't share his enthusiasm. Tom Brandon, one of the country's most prominent physical anthropologists and Ross's colleague and supposed buddy had wondered why Ross would spend time surveying slavery.

And he certainly couldn't understand anyone investigating love *and* slavery at the same time. Ross hadn't expected this reaction. He was disappointed but not at all daunted. He understood that most blacks hadn't thought of the love that existed during slavery either. But just as he was about to determine a topic for his dissertation research, he came upon an old article in a small black newspaper about a woman who said her great-grandmother had owned a book about a powerful story of love—a slave story, about love. Ross suspected the book was *Children of Grace*. He tried to track down the woman who wrote the article but couldn't; the small newspaper had folded and Ross's attempts to find the woman through local information came up empty. Anyone else would have been disappointed, but Ross Buchanan had had a childhood that he could truly measure disappointment by, so he was not swayed. Now that he knew he was on the right track all he had to do was wait for his train to come in.

But now Ross would take a leave of absence to do what he considered his life's work. He would delve into the subject of black love from past to present. The history of black love was certainly an underdeveloped area of research, and so was slavery, but he felt that *Children of Grace* would give him a better perspective on both. Ross's work was purely academic—he was, after all, a rational man, but still he hoped and prayed that Miss Cozy could help him. This "Love Project," as he'd started to call it, may have been based in logic, but it would require his faith.

Ross had always been overly serious; his early childhood hadn't given him anything to be frivolous about. He'd been shuttled back and forth from foster home to foster home until he was in his early teens, when he found a permanent home. Young Ross didn't really understand love or what it meant to have a family. His childhood had been rough, then comfortable, then over, right when he was learning how to be a child. He remembered little of his life before coming to his last foster home. But what he remembered had not been good, so he tried to forget that, too.

Over the years, Ross had learned that trying to forget something painful is like trying to ignore yourself: You're always there, and so is the pain. For a while, his painful past was a part of him, it was all he could see. His scars were both physical and emotional. At one foster home, his foster mother's boyfriend had scalded Ross. The left side of his chest and shoulder still bore the mark of what the man had said was an accident. But once Ross was inside the emergency room, he told the doctor what had really happened. Ross thought for sure that his foster mother would put the boyfriend out, and then hold the little boy and tell him how sorry she was. Instead, he learned the meaning behind the old folks' saying "If wishes were horses, everybody would ride." The woman called Ross stupid and said he had caused her to lose her money *and* her man.

Little Ross was quickly moved to another home. This time, the parents were not overtly abusive, but he soon found that neglect was just as bad. In this particular home, he was one of eight foster children of all ages and races. His foster parents, the Stanleys, were a middle-aged white couple who took pride in what they called their "colorful tribe." But their "Save the World" charade was only for the benefit of the social workers or other folks they thought important. When no one was watching, Ross and the other kids might as well have been invisible. They were forced to fend for themselves. Ross, who was one of the oldest, started to steal. He stole anything from anyone. He was caught stealing chalk from his eighth-grade teacher's desk on the day he was moved into what would be his final foster home.

Two years later, Ross realized that he had never been anywhere this long. His new mother was everything to him, and he started to call her "Mama."

One day while he and his new mother were at church, the pastor said, "All things work together for the good of God," and Ross knew exactly what he meant. His stealing had ultimately brought him into a house that had lots of love and attention. He began to blossom immediately.

As he began to grow and mature, the old folks said he had a calling on his life. "That boy's got the mark on him, he gonna be a preacher," the old church mothers would say. Ross never knew what they meant, but he had made up his mind that he'd have no part of the preacher business. He was going to make his mark *and* his money in ways that most black folks had never thought of. He planned to take the business world by storm.

3.

The Right Fit

Josephine Chambers was the kind of woman who could wear a man's shirt and make it look like her own. She preferred the feel of its cotton to all of the textures and styles available to women. She always tried on the shirts of her lovers, as if searching for the perfect fit, the one that gave off just the right scent and warmth. She didn't know exactly how she'd recognize it, but she knew that she would.

There hadn't been many lovers, but each was always surprised to see her in his shirt and became sexually aroused or selfish and territorial. Either way, they wanted her to take off their shirt. She knew that no matter their response, it wasn't about her. It was either about their need for her body, or for their space. Josephine hoped that someday, she would find a man who didn't mind sharing his shirt.

Josephine was now dreaming about a beautiful man who was about to take off his shirt. "You can have it," he said. Just as he started to unbutton it and was exposing his smooth coffee-colored skin, Josephine's alarm went off. She immediately awoke and cursed herself for forgetting that she wouldn't need her alarm. She was taking the day off.

Josephine hadn't been out of the office since her father died two years before. After his death she'd worked harder than ever, trying to fill the void that had been left in her life.

Today she would do something for herself.

Instead of staying in bed, Josephine prepared to do one of her "when-I-get-time-I'm-going-to . . ." things—a list that she'd made up to do when she had spare time. Going to a popular black bookstore in her neighborhood was at the top of her list.

Black Images reportedly had everything, and she planned to spend the day in search of several hard-to-find books. Josephine's girlfriend Peaches had said that finding a good book was like finding a good man.

"They can be real good when you start out. You want it to last forever. Then the book takes a crazy turn and you wonder what happened. You want to stop reading, but you've invested too much time. Then some other book comes along and you start the whole thing over again."

"With a real good book," Peaches had said, "you never want it to end."

Josephine remembered her friend's words and laughed to herself and thought all she was really looking for was a book.

On this Friday morning the weather was clear and mild, so Josephine decided to walk to Black Images. A good stroll always helped to clear her head and gave her a boost of energy.

Josephine had been told that she was an old soul, and that's how she felt—like she'd been here before. She didn't get those past-life feelings that her New Age friends talked about; rather she felt old, like her name.

She never liked her name. Chambers was fine—it made her think of her heart. It was Josephine that rubbed her wrong. She thought it was too white and genteel, and always made her think of an English aristocrat who knew nothing of the black folks who'd decided that Josephine would be a good name for their children. She often thought about changing it, but she knew that it would hurt her father. After all, he was the one who had named her.

"You named after your great-great-granddaddy Joe," he'd told her.

She'd always wondered why none of her brothers had been named after him. Josephine was the only girl in a house full of boys and yet she was the one to carry on the name thing.

Josephine thought her baby brother Robby should have been named after their grandfather. Josephine was an old soul, but Robby was ancient. He was serious and quiet and never liked to do kid things. He came into this world with a keen sense of justice and never participated in any childish pranks. He just didn't understand them. And the neighborhood kids didn't understand *him*. He was a tattletale right from the start. The older boys would rough him up for turning them in, but Robby didn't seem to care. "We gotta do what's right, right Daddy?" Robby would ask.

When he was fourteen, Robby told on the wrong person. He had gone to the principal and turned in a classmate for dealing drugs. The dealer was connected to bigger pushers who didn't like losing their school business. Robby was beaten, and then shot up with the junk the dealers sold. He died without ever knowing what it meant to truly be a kid.

After Robby's funeral, Josephine got up the nerve to ask her father why she, and not Robby, had been named after her great-great-granddaddy. Ashen and hollow from the loss of his son, her father looked at her and said, "Someday, baby. You'll understand someday," and then he walked away.

By the late seventies, when Josephine was a teenager, she became aware of her cultural self, her blackness, and she hated the name even more. But there was something in the way her daddy said her name that made her know she'd never change it.

Josephine, she sometimes thought to herself, *would be a perfect name when I reach seventy.*

"Go ask old Josephine, she know all kinda stuff," she imagined the neighbors would say, talking about her to their children. Until then, she decided she would continue to go by Sister, or Baby Sis, the names her brothers had given her.

Later on, when she entered college and needed a name that sounded mature but not matronly like Josephine, she chose the name Fina.

Black Images was farther away then she'd imagined. As she looked down at her watch, she couldn't believe she'd been walking for almost forty-five minutes. Even though her walk had taken her a little longer than she'd anticipated, she still got there just as the clerk was opening the door. But as early as she was, Josephine wasn't the first person there.

4.

A Chance Meeting

🔥 "Excuse me," Josephine said as she extended her hand toward the door.

"Good morning, I'm . . . hello, uh, sorry," Ross stammered. He couldn't look at her face because he was so struck by her hands.

Ross was inside the bookstore now, and found himself following the young woman. He couldn't stop looking at her hands. Were they as strong, loving, and caring as they looked? Was she? Then he noticed her eyes and her lips: glossy, dark, and sumptuous. He wanted to say something, but what could he say? He couldn't think of anything, so instead he said nothing and stood staring at her hands.

Women had always been Ross's great distraction. He was the kind of brother who needed to think he was in love, whether he was or not. But he always ended up loving the wrong kind of woman.

Ross's mother told him frequently that when you search for romance you often find disappointment, and that it took time to find real love. "Don't rush into a relationship, son, cause they end as quickly as they begin. Take your time. Take your time." Ross didn't really understand what she was saying, until he experienced it himself. Whenever the rush of love wore off, he felt as if he'd been living a lie. "Seek peace," his mother said. "When you seek peace, you'll find love."

Ross snapped to, and remembered why he was here in this bookstore, and started searching for *Children of Grace*. But as he disappeared into an aisle he made sure he kept an eye on the young woman with the magnificent hands.

5.

The Touch

The bookstore looked more like the home of a well-read scholar than it did a shop. Beautiful maple bookshelves lined every wall. Deep sofas were arranged in between shelves that were filled with new and used books. Rare books were preciously displayed in glass cases that looked as if they could have housed diamonds as well. Colorful woven rugs were crying out to be sat upon. Ross was about to ask a young clerk if she'd ever heard of *Children of Grace* when he looked down on a coffee table and noticed an old yellowed manuscript. There were just pages with no cover wrapped with an old satin ribbon to hold the pages together. Red dye from the ribbon had stained the sides of the pages. Ross thought of Al Jarreau's vocal rendition of Spain: "And all its edges folded and the corners fade to sepia brown and yet it's all I have of our past love—a postscript to its ending." Next to the pages there was a carved wooden box that looked to be the perfect size for the book. The words on the pages were difficult to make out, but something in his spirit told Ross it was the treasure he was looking for. As he approached the table and leaned down to grab the book the woman he'd run into earlier reached for the book, too.

"Excuse me, I think I had this first," she said.

She spoke with a deep, throaty sound that echoed the essence of her hands; an older seasoned voice floated out of a young body. Ross imagined that he could live forever inside the timbres of her voice.

When she saw that it was *Children of Grace* she quickly stuck her hand out against the book from the other side to make it appear she'd discovered it at that moment, too. Josephine had learned this technique from her girlfriend Peaches one day while they were outlet shopping. She'd gotten away with it before, but this was different. The person on the other end wasn't some enormous maniac who was trying to grab her size-ten skirt. Instead, there was a beautiful brown brother who looked at her as if he knew her.

"Excuse me." The young woman's tone was businesslike.

"Maybe you could ask . . . maybe *we* could ask the owner to find another copy."

He walked around the table toward her, careful not to break contact, holding a corner of the book and as much of her hand as possible.

"How is this book automatically yours?" he asked. "Didn't we both find it at the same time?"

Something about her seemed familiar to him; not in his head, but in his heart. Maybe it was the fragrance she was wearing. A deliciously light scent, soft and extremely alluring, was coming from her hair. Whoever she was, she was getting to him in a way he hadn't been touched before.

6.

Black Images

🌾 When Ross and Fina got to the counter they could see Cosina Brown, the owner of Black Images, at the far end of the shop helping a customer find what *she* thought he needed. On the wall above the counter hung a sign that read A BOOK IS A GIFT YOU CAN OPEN MORE THAN ONCE.

Cosina Brown was a tall dark woman in her sixties who looked to be no more than a day past forty. She was known to everyone as Miss Cozy; it was the name an old Puerto Rican friend had given her back when she was in her twenties.

"Do you know what your name means?" he had asked with an accent that even melted a piece of her sturdy heart.

"No, it's just a name my mother made up," she told him.

"*Cocina* is Spanish for 'kitchen,'" he said.

Cosina didn't know how to take this new information. She

had always felt awkward in her tall body, not quite comfortable, as if she were trapped in someone else's skin. She wasn't athletic, nor was she clumsy—but no one would call her graceful. Her stature was closer to a man's, but Cosina Brown was all woman.

Before she could become too dispirited by the fact that her name in Spanish meant "kitchen," the friend went on to tell her that the name fit her perfectly.

"You are cozy like a kitchen, warm and full of whatever one may need."

The friend became her lover, but only for a summer. Apparently, the kitchen didn't stock *everything* he needed, and he went on to someone else. She'd loved him and learned from him but knew in her heart of hearts that she didn't really *need* his love. Still, he had given her what she needed: a name that made her feel like herself. So from then on, Cosina went by Cozy.

Over the years, Miss Cozy had become a sage on the subject of African American literature. Her shop was a neighborhood fixture and maintained a quality selection of books reflecting everything black.

The store had been an ordinary bookshop until Miss Cozy had a vision to specialize in rare and hard-to-find books by black authors. This change put Miss Cozy's store on the map and attracted folks from across the country. People came from all over to find what could not be found anywhere else. And what surprised customers most was that they usually walked away with something they didn't even know they needed. But sometimes they just came to hear Miss Cozy talk about "her children." That's what she called her books.

In recent years, Black Images had become a popular hub for the new crop of black artists and intellectuals. It also attracted regular, everyday people who simply wanted to share Miss Cozy's space and experience her energy.

Other times people came for her recommendations. Miss Cozy had an uncanny ability to look you in the eyes and tell you what book went best with your troubles without ever hearing you say a word. This is what made her the darling of the authors themselves. It wasn't uncommon to drop by and see bestselling authors asking Miss Cozy what *they* should be reading.

Folks swore Miss Cozy's suggestions had changed their lives, or at least they'd loved the books so much they'd never wanted them to end. She could sense a connection between people and books and knew when it would be most important for those people to read them.

But this was just one of her gifts. Some said Miss Cozy had the ability to "read" people. Folks swore Miss Cozy could read their thoughts and their futures. When asked about the gift, Miss Cozy would simply avoid the question, but there was more to her than you could see. Miss Cozy's mother told her that she was born with a veil on her head. The afterbirth clung to her face like a blanket. You came sliding into this world screaming like you wanted to go back from where you came from.

Miss Cozy looked up as the couple approached the counter.

Miss Cozy watched these two, as she'd watched so many others. She knew that they had no idea how their lives were going to be affected. Other folks had come to her shop thinking that they had been led to the bookstore because of their own intuition. But she knew better. This was her purpose, her calling: to help others unfold the chapters of their lives by reading between someone else's lines.

Once a woman had come into her bookstore, and before

she could say a word, Miss Cozy told her, "*In Search Of Satisfaction* by J. California Cooper. Down two aisles on the left. Read it and come back when you're through."

A day later, the woman came back crying. She wanted to know how Miss Cozy could tell that Cooper's book was just what she'd needed. The woman said that she hadn't gotten along with her mother for years, but that by reading this beautiful story, she knew that her present troubles were connected to her past and learned that in order for her to move on, she would have to learn to forgive.

Miss Cozy told the woman that she had no idea how she knew what she knew.

"All I know is that when I listen to myself, something powerful happens," she said.

Miss Cozy was deep, and she knew it. But she was also the most down-to-earth woman anyone would come across; she knew what she knew and therefore there was no need to be haughty.

She watched this woman and man with a sense of familiarity. There was something special about them, something more. Something so powerful, that even she couldn't yet figure it out.

What she did know was that she needed them as much as they needed her, and that their lives were somehow interconnected.

She walked around the counter and smiled at them, and felt as if she were greeting close relatives she hadn't seen in a long time. Old memories came rushing back to her, and she expected either of them to call her by her childhood nickname.

"I hope you haven't been waiting too long," she said. "Now, who's first, or are you together?"

Fina took a deep breath and gathered her thoughts. Uncharacteristically, she was unsure of what she was about to say.

"Well," she stammered. "Um . . ."

Should she put her cards on the table and confess that he'd gotten to the book first, or should she make a strong appeal on her own behalf because of the book's special importance to her? But before she could say anything else, Ross cut in. "We're together."

Josephine didn't understand, but remained quiet.

"We—are—together," he repeated plainly. "Our problem

is that there's just one copy of this book and we both need it . . . unless you have another copy?"

"Um-hmm," Miss Cozy said, while reaching for the ragged pages. Miss Cozy lifted the book and began to smile. *"Children of Grace.* Hmm. Very hard to come by, very hard indeed."

A twinkle flashed in her eye as she looked at the couple.

"And why do you need two copies?" Miss Cozy knew there were no other copies, but she had to find out their intentions. Over the years, *Children of Grace*, for better or for worse, had passed through many hands. On numerous occasions it was supposed to be published, but every time, something happened. Publishers changed their minds, the book was lost or stolen. One time, a publisher who planned to get the book from its owner by less than noble means became deathly ill. The plain truth was that *Children of Grace* wasn't supposed to be distributed to a large audience before it was time. As powerful as the book was for Miss Cozy, it was destructive for others. Miss Cozy also harbored another secret about the book. One that she wasn't ready to reveal to these two or anyone else.

7.

An Introduction

🌿 "Young man," Miss Cozy said, "I asked you why such a cute couple would need two copies, and I'm still waiting for an answer."

Ross smiled at the older woman's use of the word "couple." "Well," he stammered, "we need two because we're not going home to the same place. You see, we'd like to read this book at the same time."

"So," she said, smiling slyly, "why don't you take turns reading to each other?"

Josephine broke in with an edge in her voice. "What the brother is trying to say is that *we*, he and I, are not a couple. We don't even know each other! We're both just trying to buy the same book. But if he wants it that badly, he can have it." She didn't mean it, though; she just didn't know what else to say.

Miss Cozy raised an eyebrow. She could tell that Josephine wasn't accustomed to down-home flirting, or that someone who'd flirted with her had treated her badly. *I'll have plenty of time to teach this chile a thing or two,* she thought to herself. *I don't need to do it now.*

"Y'all don't know each other, so go on and introduce yourselves."

The young woman looked at Ross and gave a curt introduction. "My name is Josephine, people call me Fina, my close friends and family call me Sister." She said it all in one breath, letting the other two know that she wanted to get the formalities over with quickly.

"Lord, chile. We ain't in a race. But thanks for the info," Miss Cozy said. "That wasn't so hard. I don't know what's wrong with you young people. Used to be in my day, you couldn't pass another black person without speaking. And if you didn't know them, you went out of your way to find out who they were. Nowadays though," she continued while sucking her teeth, "y'all use *not* knowing somebody as an excuse not to speak."

Miss Cozy turned to Ross and said, "And you? I've seen you

in here a couple of times, but you were always in a hurry. I haven't had the chance to get to know you. But I do know your name is Ross something or other."

"Buchanan," Ross replied. "Good memory, but I don't ever remember telling you my name."

"You didn't have to," Miss Cozy told him. "Once, you were in here looking for a book called *When God Was a Woman*. Not too many men request that book, so I looked at the name on the sales receipt to see who you were."

Out of the corner of his eye he could see the young woman fidgeting impatiently, waiting for her introduction.

"Oh yes, my name is Ross Buchanan. Very nice to meet you. People call me Ross, but you can call me Brother if it makes you more comfortable."

Miss Cozy was smiling, but Fina didn't see the humor. *Why is he mocking me?* she wondered.

"I'm Miss Cozy," the older woman threw in. "Well, at least that's what everybody calls me. Welcome to Black Images. Now let's cut to the chase: *Children of Grace.*

"Only one copy of this book exists, and this is it. The very fact that you two know about this book and are here at the same time is rather amazing. The only reason this old book is out is because I was rereading it last night and I forgot to put it away. I'm getting a bit older, you know . . . and before this gal gets anymore pushy thoughts, let me tell you straight up, I am *not,* by any means, no matter how necessary, selling this book."

The telephone on the counter rang and Miss Cozy excused herself to answer it. With her hands she was telling them to hold on.

"Oh Lord, yeah. Uh-huh."

But with her voice she was holding a rather one-sided conversation.

"Yes, I know what you need and I told you how long it would take. Now the truth is, I'm getting this quicker than anybody else could, so if you know what's best, you'll hold them horses of yours."

Miss Cozy gave Ross and Fina a signal that said she'd be just one more minute.

"Yes, well that's fine with me, but if you needed it sooner, you should have placed the order sooner. You just wait two more days like I told you, and come by then. And don't be sending no car either. Remember, I knew you before you could spell your own name. And speaking of names, what's this I hear about you changing *yours*? What's wrong with the one your mother gave you? You folks get a little bit famous and you forget who you are. No, my mother didn't name me Cozy, but that ain't none of your business. Two days, baby. I'm busy. Love you."

Without bothering to say good-bye, she hung up.

8.

"As We Let Our Light Shine"

Fina looked around and took in her immediate surroundings: the customers, the colors, the art, the sounds, and the man next to her.

Fina thought she might be standing beside the kind of man that women say they really want. "The kind of guy who has a sense of humor, and is able to put the needs of others first." But what most women really mean is "fine with a nice car, and even nicer bank account."

She stifled a laugh and thought, *Just who is this brother?*

Fina's common approach to life's puzzles was to figure things out first before asking a single question. Her father had said, "Men will tell you everything you need to know without ever asking. Just let 'em talk. They love to talk. They need to brag, and when they do, they let the truth out. Lotta women like to guide the conversation, but what you end up doing is getting what you want to hear, rather than what really is. Men will tell you everything. Just learn to listen and let 'em talk."

Fina owed her father a big debt. Almost everything she knew about life she'd learned from him after her mother died when Fina was twelve.

Everyone had expected her father to remarry quickly. "All them children, you need a woman around, especially for that gal," she recalled her relatives saying. As she grew older, she was regarded as a tomboy; older still, and she was thought to be a lesbian. Fina never had time for "girliness," as she called it, but she was all woman nonetheless, so there was no need for lace.

She'd sat by and watched as her friends had prepared for the debutante balls and the proms she was never invited to. The girls would go on and on about how their mothers didn't understand them. Then they'd remember Fina's presence and give fake sympathy. Fina wanted to yell at them, tell them that even if she didn't have a mother, she still had a father and had aunts that got on her nerves, too. At the same time, she wondered what it was that was missing from her life. Even though she hadn't wanted to participate in many of the major events in a girl's life, Fina didn't take to boys all that well either. True, she fought and played with her own brothers, but when the time came for dating, she just wasn't comfortable. It just all seemed so awkward. This had nothing to do with her self-esteem. She believed she was beautiful—and men were constantly telling her how fine she was—but she just didn't like the way boys treated the girls they went out with. Even her own brothers, whom she adored, were two-faced when it came to the opposite sex. She watched them be the well-mannered men her father had raised, but she listened through the wall that separated their bedroom from hers and heard their crude conversations.

When she grew older and went away to college, she wondered what the big deal was, and decided to see. After a few dates, she realized that she did like the attention and feeling that came with being admired, but Fina was fiercely independent and vowed to stay single. As protective as her brothers were of her, they were not kind to the women they dated and later married. Fina believed they wanted to do the right thing but they didn't know how. She figured that it had something to do with her mother's early death. Her oldest brother, Terrence, was eighteen when their mother passed. He had been a mama's boy, and he took her death the hardest. T, as they called him, treated every relationship as if the woman might leave him at any moment. So instead of making sure it didn't happen, he prepared himself for when it did. To say that he had a fear of commitment was an understatement: Terrence sabotaged his relationships.

In public he was Mr. Nice Guy, kind and caring, but in private he was manipulative and controlling with the women he dated. One day, when a situation with a woman he'd been dating reached a fever pitch, he took matters into his own hands. Until then he'd only been emotionally abusive. But if you open the door to emotional abuse, you might as well make a bed for physical abuse, too.

T wound up in jail. Their father refused to put up bail, and forbade any family member to do so. "I didn't raise nobody to beat no women. Let him learn that." T stayed in jail for three days before he was released. When he came home, the only thing his father said to him was, "The laws need to be changed, you shouldn't be out so quick." To Fina's knowledge, T never struck a woman again, but he continued to struggle with commitment.

On the other hand, her brother Stan was overly trusting and fell for every woman who said hello. He was constantly falling in love. "This is the one, Fina, I can feel it," he would say.

"You always say that, Stan," she replied.

"Nope, this is really it."

At first, women thought Stan was the most romantic and attentive brother they'd ever met. They were all won over by his charm and constant gift giving. But they soon learned Stan's other side, the side that wouldn't let them breathe. Stan's obsessive attention was another form of abuse. While it was the opposite of the way T treated women, the root cause was the same—the loss of a loving mother. Fina figured out that Stan was trying to hold on to the mother he had lost by smothering the women he thought he loved.

Unfortunately for Fina, watching her brothers' behavior turned her into more of a skeptic. She often quoted the line her father used whenever someone told him to remarry. "People today are crazy. I can do bad all by myself."

Fina still missed seeing her mother and father together.

They'd shared an unusual kind of love. For almost twenty years her parents were best friends. Fina missed seeing them whisper and giggle to each other. Sometimes, when they thought no one was looking, Fina's mother and father would mouth the word "later." As a girl she didn't understand her parents' special language, but when she was grown, she found out what it meant.

She tried to re-create what her parents had and wound up married to the first man who asked her. The marriage was short lived, and later she had laughed and told her girlfriends that *she*, by herself, was the perfect couple.

Her husband, although he was bright and upwardly mobile, had placed very little importance on their relationship. She marveled at how the man who had literally begged her to be his queen had no time for her once he'd won her. It seemed to her that with men, the whole relationship thing was like a game, and Fina didn't like being the prize. When Fina first told her husband that she was unhappy, he asked her why. He reminded her that he had put her on a pedestal and had chosen her above all the rest. She quickly informed him that on a pedestal there was absolutely no place to go but down.

After her divorce, Fina dated when she felt lonely, but the relationships never lasted. She'd been told that she was a "hard case." Men couldn't get close, no matter what tactics they tried. She was warm, and at times passionate, but she would not connect. Besides, she still didn't like being thought of as a case or a prize. What she disliked even more was the fact that she could feel lonely even when she was not alone. She buried herself in her work and volunteer projects. Fina felt that her life was supposed to be better than it was. She just didn't know how to make it that way.

Unable to bear Ross's eyes piercing through hers, Fina looked away and noticed a poster of Nelson Mandela. A line from his inaugural speech was written below it. Fina had seen it before, but this time it was speaking directly to her: "And as we let our own light shine, we unconsciously give other people permission to do the same. As we are liberated from our own fear, our presence automatically liberates others."

9.

When You're Ready to Learn, the Teacher Appears

🌱 "It looks like you two want to buy something that's not for sale, not at any price. Sorry, your money won't do you any good here today," Miss Cozy said. Fina felt like there would be a "but" at the end of that sentence, so she didn't jump in as she normally would have.

"People come through these doors from far and wide to find a special book, willing to spend whatever they have to. This one . . . this one," she repeated while retying the worn satin ribbon around the pages, "is not for sale under any conditions. But," the woman said, her eyes sparkling, "let's just pretend that it is for sale. What would this old book be worth to you?"

Fina kept silent. Before she said anything, she wanted to

know why Ross was interested in the manuscript. Fina assured herself it had to be a frivolous excuse.

Even though Miss Cozy was adamant about not selling the book, Fina felt it was still within her grasp. Her heart started to beat furiously in anticipation. She wasn't sure of the details, but Fina knew the book would eventually end up in her hands. She didn't need to know all the particulars.

Fina believed that God always placed two roads before us, with lots of signposts along the way. The Bible says, "He who seeks a sign, seeks calamity." Her grandmother would say, "God will give you a sign; they everywhere. So ain't no need to go looking."

Throughout Fina's life, she had noticed a favorite color here, a song there, or that nagging feeling when you're about to make the wrong choice. But as she stood in the bookstore, even though she wasn't all that comfortable, she felt she was exactly where she was supposed to be.

"So, Ross, what's the book worth to you? Is it a gift?" Fina asked.

"Yes," he answered. Then he thought, *Yeah, it's a gift—for me.*

Ross had first learned about the book many years ago from a professor. Just recently, while moving into his new home, he'd come across some grad school papers from Professor Lewis, and he stopped to read them. Lewis was a man full of wisdom, teaching would-be Ph.D.s while he didn't have one himself.

When he was in college Ross was majoring in economics and had to take a black studies course to fulfill his core requirements. And it's a good thing he was forced to take the course, because he wouldn't have taken it otherwise. At the time the only thing he thought black people needed to be concerned with was the color green: money.

But after taking the course with Professor Lewis, Ross changed his field of study to anthropology.

Professor Jeremiah Lewis was a short man with smooth unlined skin who looked to be in his early fifties. As Ross spent more time with Lewis and got to know him better he was shocked to find out that the Professor was in his seventies. After that, whenever Ross saw Professor Lewis he couldn't help think of the phrase "Black don't crack."

Lewis taught his course as if every theory and research

finding were current events. He didn't just tell you about the Underground Railroad, he made you feel what it was like to be there. Ross thought back to the day that he'd heard about the book *Children of Grace.*

Lewis had walked into the classroom, put down his bags, and closed his eyes. "For some of you, this will be one of the most important classes of your life."

For a long time Ross had been puzzled by that comment and wondered if he was one of those people. Now as he stood in Black Images, Ross felt that Professor Lewis's comment may actually be true.

"Ahem, excuse me. . . . What do you know about this book, anyway?" Fina asked Ross.

"Let's see . . ." Ross recalled. "It's said that the book was written by an enslaved woman who claimed that she could see the future. She wrote about her life and her love for a man named Joe. Everyone thought she was crazy, but what's really crazy is that before she wrote this book, she didn't know how to read or write.

"I've done some research on several people who were said to have possessed the gift of spontaneous writing. Nat Turner was one of them. Even though he credits the slave owner for having taught him to read and write, research indicates that he confided to some people that his writing came as a gift. There are numerous accounts of automatic writing among our enslaved ancestors. And I guess if one looked, there would be evidence of this in other segments of the population as well. Supposedly, this sort of thing has been known to happen in churches, too. Folks who have never played the piano in their entire lives are able to play complete songs. Some are even able to play classical music."

Fina was intrigued by this man and his knowledge, asked, "How do you know all this?"

"I'm an anthropologist, but I specialize in urban myths."

"Urban myths?" Fina asked.

"It's a relatively new field of study. Urban myths are tales or legends that have become so widespread that they're thought to be true. You know, modern-day folklore, like Candy Man. Then there was the one about Tommy Hilfiger's appearance on *Oprah*. I still get e-mail claiming that she kicked him off the stage."

Fina nodded. "Yeah, I heard that one, too. We had Bloody Mary. If you said her name five times in a mirror, she would come and kill you. I was a young girl the first time I heard that story, and I was so afraid that I couldn't walk past a mirror for months!"

"Okay, so you know what I'm talking about," Ross continued. "For a long time *Children of Grace* was believed to be precisely that—an urban myth that had become widespread. Back when I was writing my dissertation, I uncovered documents that suggested the book may actually exist. I also found a love letter that the slave Joe had written to his wife, Iona.

"Like most important artifacts, it was buried in the library. I was going through slave purchase documents when I found the letter. It was with the purchase papers for Iona's freedom. The papers had been in a fire, so I couldn't make out who the purchaser was. Seems like the closer I got to figuring this thing out, the further away I was."

"Do you have a copy of that letter, son?" Miss Cozy asked.

"Yes, ma'am. Got it right here. I made a copy of it, and I've kept it with me ever since."

Ross pulled out the copy of the letter he carried in his

wallet and read it to Fina and Miss Cozy. They were both amazed and didn't mind letting Ross know.

"I know how you feel," Ross told them. "Now that I'm seeing the book, I can hardly believe it myself. It almost seems too good to be true," Ross whispered.

Miss Cozy shook her head. "Not really. When you're ready to learn, the teacher appears."

10.

The Garden

"What I'm trying to tell you," Miss Cozy continued, "is that the trick to getting what you want in life is all about balance. You have to first understand the difference between needs and wants. You have to work on what you need, and balance your life so that when you get what you want, you don't go making another list of needs." Miss Cozy paused for a second. "And it seems like today is your lucky day." She smiled and moved toward the back of the shop. "Come along, I'd like to show you something."

She led the couple through the store to a rear exit, which opened onto an outdoor patio. Ross and Fina were astonished to see rows of colorful flowers growing right in the middle of the city. Miss Cozy's garden was beautiful, secluded and serene. There were vegetables that looked like they belonged in the

South. Red tomatoes and collard greens that Fina would kill for grew neatly in the same kinds of rows that she'd seen at her grandmother's house. Two handmade rocking chairs were nestled in the shaded area of the patio. Miss Cozy saw Fina staring at them.

"Those chairs belonged to my great-great-uncle. He made 'em during slavery time and they were passed on to me."

Miss Cozy's thoughts drifted back to the first time she had seen the chairs. As a young girl, when her family was visiting her mother's folks down south, she remembered her father arguing with her mother. Their voices were trying to whisper, but their tones were yelling.

"We ain't taking that old shit nowhere near my house."

Cosina always hated when her father referred to things that belonged to them as his. He was a hardworking and proud man, but his pride was not always a good thing. Cosina's family was one of the "First Negroes To," as she called them.

"We were the first negroes to do this, and the first negroes to do that," she recalled.

Her father was a doctor, and her mother was a nurse, and they were the first to move to their white Cleveland suburb.

For most of her life, her father wanted to leave the past behind. For many years their home had been decorated like something out of *Better Homes and Gardens*. Cozy was always dressed like a little lady—and in those days, little lady implied little white lady. Cosina was never comfortable in her black middle-class life. The black part she was happy with; it was the middle class that she couldn't stand. She didn't like being in the middle. It was too easy to see what was on either side, and usually, it was somebody who didn't want any part of you.

Her mother and father argued about those chairs, or rather her father argued and her mother listened. Her father won, and her beloved chairs had to stay right there with her grandmother. Cosina thought that one of her relatives must have seen the way she sat in those chairs and realized how much they meant to her. Every day, she would talk to them and rock herself to sleep.

Long after her father had passed away, and after she had opened her book shop, Cosina received a large delivery. She was surprised to see the chairs that she had forgotten about. There was a note attached from her second cousin that said that she'd been instructed by some old crazy neighbor to give Cosina the chairs instead of throwing them out. Cosina remembered Miss Berty, the woman who lived across the road. Miss Berty would wave at Cosina and call her to "come and sit," as she called it. She told Cosina stories of the old folks and told her to always be proud of her people.

She said, "No matter where you live or how you live, you gonna always be colored. That's a good thing," she said. "Being colored might not mean much now, but one day it will. Oh, it will."

The woman was old when Cosina was a child. She thought, *She must be a hundred by now.* However old she was, Miss Cozy was happy that she had survived long enough to see that the chairs made it back to her—their rightful owner.

Miss Cozy had been eager to talk with Miss Berty and hear the many stories she undoubtedly still had to tell. Cosina was going to make a trip South to interview her, but when she called her cousin, she learned that Miss Berty had died in her sleep the night before. Miss Cozy wept for Miss Berty, but mainly she cried for the history, the untold stories, the truths that died with her.

"I come out here to escape," she said to Ross and Fina. "Sitting here works wonders. Go 'head, try it out," she said.

Fina sat down first. She smoothed her hand across the surface of the magnificently crafted chair, enjoying its rich and sturdy bones.

"This is wonderful!"

"Let me see," Ross said while moving the other chair next to her. "Yep! I may never get up!"

"Well, enjoy! How about some iced tea?" Miss Cozy offered.

"Yes ma'am," Ross said, his voice taking on a drawl that went farther South than he had ever been.

"Two, please!" Fina added.

Miss Cozy promptly returned with two bottles of iced tea and handed them over.

"Now, I know you weren't expecting homemade!"

Ross and Fina turned abruptly as the screen door burst open and then slapped shut. A young assistant came to tell Miss Cozy that she was needed inside.

"Lord, what do I pay you for?" she asked half jokingly. "Sit back and relax, good people. Be right back."

11.
Ancient Memories

Miss Cozy left and came back almost immediately, book in hand. Without a word, she placed it on the table beside them and went back inside.

"So," Ross began, "you never bothered to say why you wanted the book."

He watched Fina's face because it was the polite thing to do, but he was thinking about her hands. He wanted to hold them, to touch the undersides of them. He wanted to feel her wrist and check to see if her pulse matched his own.

"There's something about you," he said. "Something familiar that I can't quite put my finger on. I know I've never met you, because I would have remembered. It's almost as if you're a distant relative or something."

He stared at her and after a moment he closed his eyes and

searched his mind for the place where the memory of her lived. He'd heard Southern folk talk about "ancient memories," memories that have been passed down from the ancestors reminding us of all that they wanted us to know.

Ross had found a reference to the concept of ancient memories, in Julie Dash's film *Daughters of the Dust*, the story of a family's move from the island off the coast of Carolina to the mainland, the matriarch had refused to go, but she wanted her offspring to take the ancient memories with them. Ross believed that these memories of the ancestors live on in us when we experience déjà vu.

Ross would some day do further research on the subject of ancient memories, but for now, his passion was the Love Project. He wanted to delve into black love deeper, figure out how to get black folks together again; Ross knew that when the past was uncovered, the present would become clearer.

Years before, when he had found a safe haven in his foster mother's home and observed the relationship between his mother and her boyfriend, Manny, Ross felt that nothing had more impact than true love. From Manny he learned that the most radical thing that he or any other black man could do was to love a black woman, to care for her and restore her to her rightful position in life. To erase the psychological scars of abuse left by slavery, to tenderly wipe away the disappointment from men who said that they'd be there but couldn't. Black men needed to love black women and their children and raise strong families.

But somewhere between heartbreaks and betrayals, he'd lost this vision. Now, here in the solitude of the bookstore's magnificent patio, his vision was coming back to him as if it had never left.

Ross looked at Fina again and said, "Well, my beautiful sister, are you going to tell me or not?"

She gave him a look that said she had no idea what he was talking about.

"Why do you need the book?"

Fina didn't want to say anything just yet. She was afraid that it might make her vulnerable to him, and she hated being vulnerable almost as much as she hated being lonely.

Fina grew up hearing her father talk about this book about a woman and her man who in slavery time carried the old ways from Africa and passed them down to the next generation. They were spiritual and powerful people.

Iona and Joe. Or Old Black Joe, as the plantation owner called him. Joe was a blacksmith. Fina's father explained that the blacksmith was one of the most important folks on the plantation. To the white folks, they were just skilled moneymakers, but to other blacks, they were the keepers of the history. Most blacksmiths held the information and very often the keys to freedom, both figuratively and literally. Iona was a healer, and they said she could read the stars.

"I can't remember why or how it all went down," Fina's father had said, "but before it did, Iona wrote *Children of Grace*. She didn't give it that name. Other folks who read it did. That was around the Harlem Renaissance period."

"Anyway, the book was passed down from one family member to the next and it came down to us. Somebody lost it in a stupid bet, but we still tell the story," her father said.

Fina thought all of this was just a story he'd made up for her.

When Fina was a little girl, her father always told her stories in which she was the main character. Her favorite was "Josephine for President." She could remember the dreamy look her father got whenever he told these stories. "Once upon a time, in a far faraway place," he'd begin, "there lived a little girl named Josephine. Now, Josephine was the nicest girl in all the forest. . . ."

After her mother died, he only told her stories on birthdays and special occasions. When he started telling the story of *Children of Grace*, Fina was in her early teens and not as interested as she had been when she was a little girl. Now she wished she had been. She wondered how much of this important book she had missed. Now she tried to remember exactly what her father had told her, so she made the same dreamy face she'd seen him make and recited what she could remember.

"That old woman's book was something," Fina said out loud.

Two years before, Fina's father complained of chest pains. Three days later he died. While he was making his transition, he told her that he was proud of her.

"Make sure you find your place," he whispered.

Fina still wondered what he meant. She was at the top of her advertising firm, and made more money in a month than he did in a year.

"Hello . . . is anybody home?" Ross asked Fina.

"This means everything," she said in a whisper.

"Excuse me?" Ross asked.

"This means everything," she repeated. Only this time, she spoke loud enough for him not only to hear her words but to feel them as well.

Even though he didn't understand why, he wanted to hold her, to tell her that whatever it was would be alright. The hands that had first caught his eye were now clasped together desperately in her lap, and several tears rolled down her cheeks. Slowly he reached over and placed her hands in his, enveloping her small but sturdy fingers in the warm hollow of his hands.

Ross and Fina sat for a while in the stillness of the patio. Ross felt so comfortable he wanted to sit here forever. Instead, he waited until Fina had stopped crying, picked up the old book, and started to read aloud.

12.

Charge It to My Head,
Not My Heart

Ross and Fina read the same section Miss Cozy had read the night before, and were immediately swept in. The loss of Iona's mother was something that Fina and Ross, both orphans, could identify with. Ross paused and looked over at Fina. She was struggling to look composed but Ross could still detect a thin veil of pain.

Miss Cozy walked back outside and sat down. She loved this old book, and couldn't help listen to the story again. Miss Cozy found herself remembering when she first got the book and what it had meant to her.

Unlike these two, she hadn't had any idea of what this book was about. Cosina had all the so-called luxuries that any middle-class black child of the forties and fifties could want. But her suburban Cleveland home lacked the love she felt when she visited her mother's family down South. Her father, the good black doctor, flaunted his numerous affairs and her mother turned to alcohol. By the time Cosina was in college, she, too, was known to have more than the occasional drink.

The college years were challenging for Cosina and she spent most of her time running from one boyfriend to the next and hanging out late. Still her natural curiosity and love for knowledge allowed her to maintain a low B average, so no one identified her as being out of control. But she was.

The summer of her junior year in college, her grandmother asked her to come down South. Cosina had already decided to take a trip to Europe and told the old woman so. When she got back, her grandmother had passed away several days before. At her grandmother's going-home service, Miss Berty pulled Cosina aside. She had been staring at her the entire day, and Cosina, who couldn't look Miss Berty in the eye, was ashamed. She should have been there for her grandmother, but instead she'd thought only of herself. It was as if Miss Berty had read the young woman's thoughts. She pulled

Cosina to her and held her. "It's alright child, we can only do what we've been taught."

Cosina wept for the grandmother who showed her true love, and she cried about her own selfishness. Miss Berty smiled and said, "That's alright, baby. It's been charged to your head, not to your heart."

During the next few weeks, Cosina stayed and organized her grandmother's things. Her grandmother had left instructions that Cosina and Cosina alone was to distribute her belongings.

The old woman had left a scrupulously detailed note consisting of an itemized list of her possessions, as well as a list of what should go to whom. Her grandmother had worked for the wealthy families in town, and over the years had been given many precious antiques. All of these items went to other relatives, and when everything had been parceled out, Cosina was shocked to find that all she received was an old book.

Surely there had been a mistake.

But inside of the book Cosina found a note:

My Dearest Cosina,

You're old enough now to know the expression "Many are called, few are chosen." Well, you are one of the chosen.

Right now, your life is all over the place. You haven't figured out who you are, or why you were born. Don't fall into the same temptations your mama did. Money and men are easy to get, but they easy to lose, too. Wisdom will stay with you always. This book was supposed to come to your mama, but she lost her way in life when she married your daddy. Now you have to pick up what she left undone. I wanted to tell you this face to face, but I didn't have no more time to do it.

This book is for you and no one else. Not yet, anyway. It holds the Recipe of Life. You know from watching me cook that the recipe is only half of the cake. The cook has to know how to bring the right ingredients together. Cosina, the ancestors chose our family to be the cook. You gotta get this to the right ones. It's only for them. I don't know how you'll know, but when the time comes, you will.

I wished I could teach you more, but the book will tell you what I couldn't.

I'll be in that Cloud of Witnesses watching over you.

I love you, my little Coco,

Grandma

Months after her grandmother's "transition service," as her mother called it, she was still puzzled by the note. She wondered why no one had heard of this book before if it was so important. Before she even bothered to read it, Cosina took the book to a rare bookstore to have it appraised, only to be told that it had no real value.

Aside from being old, the white appraiser told her, it looked to be like any other family journal.

"This book," he said, "only has value for your people." The emphasis the appraiser had placed on the word "your" left an indelible mark on Cosina.

In shorthand he was saying that anything of importance to a black family would not have any real monetary or other value to anyone else.

She was shocked by his attitude. From the moment she'd

walked in the store, the owner had looked at her as if she didn't belong there.

Now she was thankful for that exchange with the appraiser. If he'd taken Cosina seriously—taken the book seriously and actually read it—he would have known its worth. She was so glad she'd held on to the book. After she'd read it, she realized that no sum of money could ever convince her to let the book go.

When she finally got over her disappointment with her grandmother and read *Children of Grace*, Cosina could see what a precious gift she'd been given.

Her grandmother had always said nothing ever happens before its time, and she was right. The book sat on Cosina's bookshelf for years before she read it. She couldn't even remember what finally prompted her to investigate its musty pages. But life was like that. Truth only comes when you're ready to face it.

Most folks go through their entire life working day in and day out, completely happy in the simplicity of paying bills. The idea that they are here for something greater barely crosses their minds. On the rare occasion when these people allow themselves to dream and imagine what their lives could really be like if they took a risk, there is usually someone there to remind them that dreams don't come true.

These people never find their purpose, their calling. These are the folks whose grandchildren and great-grandchildren are burdened with the unfulfilled longings of their ancestors. Cosina often listened to her authors debate the problems facing black America. They talked about "vicious cycles" and black-on-black crime like they invented these concepts. Cosina saw that the roots went deeper and that "vicious cycle" was just a fancy way of saying "generational curse." She'd opened her bookstore to show that black folks were a blessed people and that they only had to see it for themselves, read about it for themselves.

Once Cosina had read *Children of Grace*, or better yet, the book had read her, she understood clearly what she was here to do. It was then that she took on the task of selling powerful and sometimes rare books. The day after she'd finished the book, Cosina started to hear things and became more aware of everything around her. She'd planned to spend the afternoon with her boyfriend that day. When he finally arrived, Cosina was amazed to find out that she could tell when he was lying to her about where he had been. She didn't understand what was happening to her, why she was reacting this way, but her feelings were too potent to ignore. Not knowing what to do, she confronted him with what she'd seen. At first he denied it, but she was much too accurate for him to continue in his denial. He accused her of being some kind of a witch and ran off. Cosina never heard from him again.

Her new abilities put a strain on most of her relationships. It was only when she began to sell her special books that she was able to be at peace.

Ross and Fina were more than ready. Cosina could see in their eyes that they'd been searching. During her life she'd learned that many folks are in search of the truth without knowing it. They may think that what they need is a mate or a big house, lots of friends, or even the power to influence. Their search, however, is for truth—that truth being the simple understanding of who we are and why we're alive. One of Cosina's favorite authors, psychologist Naim Akbar, talked about the importance of asking questions like "Why me, here, now? What am I here for, and what was I called to do?" Asking was the first step toward finding out.

Miss Cozy had a feeling that this woman and man who had come in alone would leave together, and find all that they needed. She could read the signs pointing to the road of truth all over life's highway. They were in the songs of Oleta Adams, Aretha Franklin, Roberta Flack, and Nina Simone. Nancy Wilson learned lessons echoed from Jimmy Scott and Billie Holiday, the Duke, the Count and King Brown, Little Richard and Trane.

Miles played the truth, even if he couldn't get it right for himself.

Filmmaker Gordon Parks had led the way and passed the torch to Bill Dukes, who in turn shared it with Julie Dash, Euzhan Palcy, Peter Bratt, and Forest Whitaker.

The written word was full of signs from everyone from Douglass to Thurman to Zora to Baldwin. These were the writers who'd stumbled onto the truth, but deliberately taught it to others. And then came Octavia Butler, LeRoi Jones, and Alice Walker, A J Verdelle, LeVar Burton, Barbara Neely, Michael Eric Dyson, Cornel West, Wright, both Richard and Jeremiah,

Johnny Ray Youngblood, Haki Madhabuti, Paulo Coehlo, Naim Akbar, and so many others.

Road signs leading to the truth were everywhere. But most folks didn't see them. People look to organized religion as a means to find truth. And even when trouble stares them in the face, they reduce it to a feeling or an escape from life, rather than a way through it. They use their religion as a means to oppress, when the truth was meant to liberate all.

Miss Cozy felt that for most black folks, religion had become another outlet for drama.

Miss Cozy thought of all the books she had read and sold. She thought of the joy they brought and smiled. Now the book *Children of Grace* was across from her in the hands of a young man who would also see its power.

Miss Cozy took the book from Ross. He must have thought that she was going to put an end to the reading, because he jumped for the book like his life depended on it.

Miss Cozy knew that it did.

"Calm down, young man," she told Ross. "You need a break. And since I'm closing up, I've decided to read to you for a while."

She sat down and shifted her weight in a big soft chair that looked as if it had been made to fit her.

"Every time I read this book, it's like reading it for the very first time. Let's see," Miss Cozy said while adjusting her reading glasses. "Where did you all leave off?"

Ross leaned in to show Miss Cozy, and when he did, the light smell of sweet milk filled the air. Fina smelled it, too, but didn't say a word. Miss Cozy just smiled and said, "Y'all ready?" and she began to read.

13.

Freedom Talk

I try not think about my mama. It was some time before I even knew that I didn't have one. My daddy, the man who raise me, didn't tell me about her right away.

I was a different chile. That's cause my daddy, the man who raise me, gave me all the love he had. So much that I never thought that none was missing. Some folks got a way of giving a chile so much love that they never know how bad things really is. My daddy was like that.

When I was a girl, I would run around talking bout how someday I was gonna be free. I tell my daddy, we was all going to be free and that nobody would own us. I say, "Daddy, if you want, you'll be able to have a wife and that woman can be my mama and she can be free, too." Daddy just smile, and I know he love my free-dom talk. That's what he call it. We never talk like this when nobody else was around. Daddy say not to. But it make him happy when I do it.

He come in most days from making shoes for horses and other stuff that old man Hunn was going to make money from and I sing my freedom song. "We gone be free, we gonna be free, all us here gonna be free." Then I make Daddy sing. He had a big old voice that everybody love to hear. His voice could do anything. It made folks know when Mr. Hunn was coming and it would tell them if a baby was borned or if somebody die. Even if they live on another plantation way down the road, my daddy would know and would sing bout it. He sing in what they call a code. Sometimes he singing bout a chicken and a rooster, but that mean man and woman. If he singing bout the lazy dog, he telling where the white folks is. When Daddy say that dove flew down the road, we know somebody dead. Wasn't no white person who knew what Daddy was saying either. They just thought he was always happy.

One day, I was in the barn with him when he was working, I was happy to watch my daddy work, so I start singing my freedom song. All a sudden, my daddy, the man who raise me and love me, haul off and slap me hard right on the face.

I ain't have no idea of what was going on, but something told me not to cry and not to say a word. I can't say nothing cause I figured there wasn't nothing to say. My daddy always tell me, "Girl, if you ain't got nothing good to say, don't say nothing."

Even though I tried not to cry, those tears came on anyway. Big tears, but still not big enough to hide in.

Til then I never been hurt by my daddy or nobody who looked like me. Looking back, I guess other folks knew what I been through, and ain't want to put nothing else on me.

The truth about my mama been kept back from me. I look at my daddy and he looking like he didn't even know me. Then he say, "How many times I got to tell you, chile, that we lucky to be where we is?"

I ain't know what he was talking about, so I ain't say nothing.

He say, "Ever time I go to town, them folks on other plantations say how they wished they could live over here."

Now I'm working to keep my mouth shut, cause I know that ain't my daddy talking.

All a sudden, young man I Iunn come in and say in a voice that's trying to be his daddy, "Why you so right. This is the best plantation anyone has ever seen, and I'm so glad you know it."

Then he look at me like we ain't never played together and said, "Now, where is my horse?"

That boy was only about ten, but he was talking to my daddy like he was some big man.

I knowed that there was nothing I could say or do. Later on that night my daddy tell me bout my real mama and how she die.

He said that Mr. Hunn was gonna kill me, too, but he beg him not to. My daddy had told old man Hunn that he would train me from a chile up to be his help and he could make double the money.

Old Hunn say okay, but if I ever turn out to be like my real mama, he gonna sure nough get rid of me. My daddy told me this on that same day that he hit me.

I hear him and think, I wish he'd just hit me again.

After the day my daddy hit me, things weren't the same no more with me and him. Not cause he hit me. He had to show that Hunn boy that he was controlling me so I won't be sold away. Even though I was just a lil girl, I understand all of that. Being a slave mean you grow up quick. Things change cause I know he wasn't my blood daddy. Seem like all the love he give me shoulda been enough. If I knowed then what I know now, it woulda been. But I was a chile who felt like I ain't have no blood roots.

I couldn't call nobody by they name. I wondered if they even knew who I was.

From that day on I pray that I can get a family of my own. That I would be they blood roots and they would call on me for guidance.

I prayed and prayed, but some things are just easier to say.

14.

It Takes a Village

Miss Cozy stopped reading and closed her eyes and the book. She didn't move for a while. Ross and Fina wanted to say something but neither could think of anything to say. Ross had always looked at history from an academic perspective. Now he was *feeling* the things he had learned. Fina was thinking of the loss of her own parents, and how achingly alone she sometimes felt without them. When her father had died several years before and she lost her remaining parent, the lights had gone out. Fina felt that there was no one left in the world who was obligated to love her, no one who would love her unconditionally. Her brothers loved and cared for her, but it wasn't the same as the love of a parent. Her brothers would eventually fill their lives with girlfriends, wives, and children. No children depended on Fina for that love either. Fina was starting to feel sorry for herself when Miss Cozy came out of what appeared to be a trance.

"Well, children, it's time for us to move ahead. Ya'll need to use the facilities?" Miss Cozy asked.

Ross wanted to smile, but instead he said, "No, ma'am."

"What about you, young lady?" Miss Cozy asked.

"Uh, no, ma'am," Fina said, imitating Ross.

"Uh-hmm," Miss Cozy said. "Well, let me see where was I? Right . . ."

I was getting to be older and more chores are put on me. There was a woman name Miss Miella, she kinda take me like a daughter. She say I look like a chile she would have if she could. I heard that Miss Miella couldn't have no babies on account of something old man Hunn and a bunch of his friends do to her. I don't know what it was, and I weren't supposed to hear that, but I was sitting round the old people one day, they were quilting, and they forgot I was there. They go to talking grown and I learn more than I should have.

By the time they remember me, I lost another bunch of good

memories. Something about bad memories that can drive your joy away.

Anyhow, Miss Miella say her mama didn't belong to nobody. She was a free Indian woman. She somehow got with her daddy, who was free, too. He was black, though. They got caught with a bunch of runaway slaves and they took 'em all up, free or no. Wasn't nothing nobody could do about it. It's a terrible thing to taste freedom, and then not have it. Must have been even harder on them to have to live like somebody else tell them to.

Miss Miella know how to do all kinda stuff. She know which plants cure what ails and how to make any kind of food taste good. She start to teach me what she know. She say, "Iona, you a good learner, you borned with the things I have to be taught." I used to go out picking plants and things with her. Sometimes I pull something and say, "What's this Miss Miella?" She'd say she didn't know but look like something her mama show her. I take that plant and boil it up, make a paste or juice with it. Seem like the plants would just tell me how to use them. I don't mean they talk to me. I ain't never seen no talking plant. But what I need em for just come to me.

Sometimes somebody get sick right after I find a new plant. I try it on myself to see if it safe. Most always it work. The worse it did was to make them sleep, and I guess that's what they need, too. Other times, though, I just mess round and come up with stuff. I even use my plants on the animals and made them better.

Miss Miella say I'm a natural doctor, but I just laugh. Who ever hear of a slave being a doctor? She teach me to read the stars, too. What they stand for, and how to find freedom when I'm grown enough. That's when I start to talk to them. Seem like they talk back. I know they don't, but in a way, it's like I'm talking to God.

Miss Miella try to get me to be happy, but I just couldn't. Truth was, I was afraid to be. I was afraid that my joy would bring back more bad.

I was about fifteen or so then. Never know my real age or the day I was borned, for that matter. My blood come, so I was starting to be a woman.

Plus that Hunn boy was looking at me more now. When we were little kids we play together, but not since that day my daddy hit me was I round him again.

Me and the other kids would be playing, but if we see him coming we just stop. He act worse than his daddy. We never spect anything good from old man Hunn, and that's just what we got. But, some of the older women hope that "the boy," as they call him, would have some sense. They nurse him and raise him. But I guess none of that matters when it comes to black and white.

Anyway, he was looking at me hard like he gonna do something. My daddy get real watchful like and try to keep me away from him. He see what's happening. Whenever that boy was around, my daddy say, "Iona, you know you got your chores. Go get to em."

I ain't know why that boy was hanging round me so. I mean I know what he want. I just didn't know why. Seem like to me, with all the freedom in the world, and black folks to do all your work, you wouldn't need nothing else from them.

Once I heard Miss Miella say that white men weren't happy unless they could own your very soul. She said they had to be sure that you knew they were in charge, cause in they heart, they knew they wasn't. I told her I didn't understand.

She say, "Iona, if you had a chile and the chile did all the work, the cooking, cleaning, then built your house. If that chile make you happy when you need them to, and take care of all of your problems, would you still think you was the mama?"

Then I know just what she meaning. She saying that them Hunns know that we really better than they tell us we is.

I thought about this hard. I wonder why we didn't see it that way. I want to tell all the folks on that plantation so we could burn down that place and start a new one but I don't do nothing. My freedom talk had got me into trouble before. I wasn't bout to bring on no more. I hear about what happen to folks when they try to raise up.

Then, too, I know what happen to my own mama.

That boy keep looking at me and trying to sneak around. My daddy stay closer and closer. He didn't even want me looking for plants by myself, so I lost that, too.

Most of the girls my age already had at least one baby. A lot of them was lily white. Old man Hunn wasn't messing around too much, but his sick friends came by. So did that boy. What he couldn't do, his friends try to.

One day, I was out with Miss Miella and three of them come up on us sudden. She tell me to run home and I did. I wish I hadn't though. Cause that was the last time I see her and I never get the chance to tell her thanks for being a mama to me. Whatever they did to her I don't know, and I tell you like my daddy tell me—some things just best not to know.

Mr. Hunn say he had to sell her cause she was causing trouble. But I know that ain't true, cause she'd a try to say good-bye to me or somebody and nobody hear a word. I tell my daddy what happen and he say I better not speak on it no more.

My life was too young to have all that inside me. I know it now, but it don't matter no more.

Shortly after that, the Hunns got hold of some money. They must have, cause they had a new batch of folk come in to work. I knew it the first day I saw him that he was special to me. Joe was older than me by about six or seven years and he was the blackest man I ever see. He have funny markings on his face, and later I learn that his mother put them there. She was pure Africa.

I would say he was beautiful, but there was something hard about his eyes. They were real sad and kinda empty. He work longside my daddy and in the field. He work real hard and didn't seem to care. He never say much to anybody, but he talk with my daddy. My daddy had that way about him. I found out that Joe wasn't his name, but I can't even say the name his mama give him. It was a

Africa name. It was pretty to hear, though. Sound like crickets talking in the night.

One day my daddy say something that make Joe smile. I never know teeth can be so pretty, specially on a man. Up til now, I never know teeth could change a face. When he laugh his eyes wasn't hard no more. They still kinda empty, though. I wasn't sure what love was then. All I know is he making me feel like myself.

He catch me staring at him and he look right at me. Truth be told, he look through me. Later on, he tell me that all he see was pain. I wished that it wasn't so. Then he could have seen my heart smiling back at him.

Anyway, my daddy see this too. All he did was smile and say he need to get something. This the first time my daddy ever leave me alone with a man. I didn't know what to say or do, so I follow after my daddy. Before I know it, Joe caught me by the arm and pull me close to him. I feel like a fool telling you bout it. But I commence to crying for my mama. Joe must of thought I was crazy cause he just laugh some more. There I was loving his laugh and wanting my mama all at the same time.

He kiss me and all I know is that I don't want to be kiss by anybody else. I never feel anything like that before. Feel like I had swallowed the sun and taste the rain. I was all warm inside. Not warm like with fever, but warm with life. It was my life coming back to me, telling me who I am, and how I fit into things. The kiss wern't that long, but it was forever for me.

I ain't know what to do. I wanted to cry and tell Joe thank you for giving me my life back, but it feel like I forget how to talk. All I could think to do was run. I don't even know why. Part of me just feel free, and part of me need to really be free. So I just run. I run fast, cause I had joy back. More than I had ever felt.

I run far from the house. Out to the fields where I find my plants. I tell myself I'm gonna get some flowers to make a oil to put in my hair, so every time Joe come near me, he'll want to kiss me some more. I sit down to get those flowers and I must have fall asleep dreaming about those kisses. I thought I could feel Joe holding me, when I know something is real wrong. When I come to myself, that Hunn boy is on top of me. He acting like my dreams was for him. He say he know that I was gonna see the light. He say it's time for me to earn my keep.

When he say that, I could hear my dead mama telling me why she had to be free.

After he did what he been wanting to do, he thank me for saving myself for him and told me to go wash. He say I smell like a pig.

Miss Cozy stopped reading and Fina began to weep.

Ross thought of all the women he knew who'd been raped or molested. For a while it seemed like an epidemic. Every other woman he came in contact with held that secret baggage; but the bags hadn't been packed by some slave master or someone of a different color, it was usually a relative, close family friend, or sometimes, it was a boyfriend or husband.

Ross was beginning to understand the personal pain that black women carried. They were still nursing the scars of ancestors who'd never known safety. He wanted to understand, but didn't think he'd ever be able to understand completely. His pain was deep, but this was something else.

He went over to Fina and held her. He rocked her in his arms for some time and they wept together.

Fina had been thinking about the time her father's friend had tried to touch her. She begged him to stop, but he kept trying. "Girl, I just want to give you something good," he said.

Her father walked into the room before his hand could go any farther.

Fina still had nightmares about it. What might have happened if her father hadn't come in? She never told her father, and she was sure he didn't know. The man still came around, but she never allowed herself to be near him. Now, whenever she was with someone who's character turned out to be less than what she expected, she thought of that man promising to give her "something good."

Miss Cozy looked at her and read her thoughts. "I know this is hard, chile, but we got to move ahead," Miss Cozy said to Fina. "It's time for you all to rest. Be here bright and early tomorrow morning."

15.

Going Home

As soon as Ross hit the pavement outside the store, he was aware of how long they had been at Black Images. "Would you like to get some coffee?" Ross asked Fina.

"Sure," Fina said. Ross wanted to clap his hands and scream, "yes!" It was after seven o'clock and Ross's favorite coffee shop was only open for breakfast and lunch.

"What's up?" Fina asked, seeing the look of dismay on Ross's face.

"My favorite coffee shop is closed," he said. "They have the best latte in town."

Then Fina said, "That's too bad, isn't it?"

She stopped dead in her tracks and brother did the same. She looked at him as if she were trying to figure something out.

"Then you changed your mind?" Ross asked.

"Not at all," Fina said. "I'm just trying to make sure you are who you say you are."

"And who would that be?" Ross asked her.

Fina said, "Just this together brother who understands the importance of history. Is that really you?"

Ross smiled and said, "That would be me."

"Okay then," she said, "follow me."

"Where to?" Ross wanted to know.

"Don't worry, I won't kidnap you," Fina said. "I know a place that makes a mean latte, and if you're nice, they may even throw in a sandwich."

"Then," Ross said, realizing what Fina was doing, "you *are* trying to kidnap me."

Fina smiled. "And I didn't even need to use a gun."

"Well, let me tell you now," Ross said, "I am not into the handcuff thing either."

Fina stopped and planted her right hand on her right hip. Ross was old enough to know that he was about to be told off.

Before Fina could say a word, he put both hands in his pockets and held his head as low as he possibly could and gave her the most sheepish look she'd ever seen. This was the sign for "I'm sorry."

Fina tried hard to ignore his pitiful plea for mercy. "Look, man," she said, trying to be stern without laughing, "I said latte, and maybe a sandwich. Nothing more. Don't even think that something is going to happen between us, because—"

Before she could finish, Ross grabbed her hand from her hip and moved in toward her. He had that "Come here, woman" look in his eyes. Ross wrapped both her arms behind her, and held Fina closely. He was standing over her and looking directly into her eyes. He held her like this for what seemed to be a long time. Ross finally broke the silence. "Look, woman," he said. "My mother had a saying: Don't start no *sh*, won't be no *it*."

Fina tried again to hold back her laughter, but couldn't. She laughed loudly, which made Ross laugh with her. Her laughter was the best he'd heard in a long while. After her laughter calmed down to a chuckle, Ross looked back into her eyes.

He was thinking about how it would feel to kiss Fina. Fina

was thinking about what it would be like to be kissed by Ross. But neither did anything. They stood there holding each other for a little longer. Then they walked hand in hand and talked about nothing and everything.

A rush of good feelings greeted Ross the instant he set foot into Fina's house. The smells he'd come to love in his foster mother's house swirled in his mind. He could almost smell his mother's fried chicken and homemade biscuits.

The vibe of Fina's house must have been what Alex Haley felt when he was received by the African village of his ancestors, and was welcomed home as if he had been that boy who'd gone off to make the drum.

The living room was splendidly decorated. There were no matching pieces. There was an overstuffed sofa with exquisite upholstery that looked both elegant and comfortable, and a modern chair next to an antique table, but everything went well together. There were African artifacts everywhere. The masks, woodcarvings, and tapestries were the glue that brought it all together. The art included works that ranged from bold photographs that made political statements to simple lithographs of young children. And there was color everywhere. Her house looked like it belonged in a magazine, but instead of the cold, "you can't sit here" feeling, it was warm and inviting.

"Oh, very nice," Ross said, examining a wooden carving of a musician. Not really knowing what else to say, Ross asked, "What kind of music you listen to?"

"Everything—as long as it's good," Fina replied.

"Me, too," Ross said, feeling like a high school boy.

He looked at the mantel over the fireplace and saw several framed photos. He could tell right away by the obvious resemblances which were family.

Many shared Fina's large oval eyes. Others had her mouth, but in none of the pictures could he see those hands he couldn't seem to let go of. He tried to keep holding them, but Fina was moving away.

She gave him a look that said "I'll be back," and went to open the doors of an antique mahogany armoire that had been converted into an entertainment center.

"Help yourself. You mind?" she asked.

She excused herself to the kitchen to make the coffee and was glad only to discover a few dirty dishes.

In her absence Ross put on Keith Jarrett's *Köln Concert*, *Side*

One. Fina smiled hearing the music—the one piece of music that could get her through anything. She studied it in college, and cried to it when her father died. She played it when she celebrated job promotions, and shared it with friends who knew the importance of background sound. The album had been recorded in the late seventies, but by the early eighties, Fina had worn out two copies. By the nineties she'd bought it on CD and had already replaced one of those.

Even though she'd listened to *Köln Concert* thousands of times over the years, every time she heard it, Fina would get lost in the music. She thought Jarrett must feel the same way because between the light melodies and the syncopated rhythms, you could hear Jarrett moaning in sweet release. In her mind, Fina had composed many fan letters to him; she wanted to thank him for expressing what she couldn't say. Now maybe she would finally put pen to paper and write Jarrett a note. How had Ross selected this album—one of her favorites—from the hundreds of CDs in her armoire? She wasn't looking for a sign, but surely, this was one.

For the first time in quite a while, Ross was aware of his second mind, the place where his true consciousness lived. It had something to do with the fragrance that floated through Fina's apartment.

It was the same scent he had noticed in Fina's hair when he first met her that morning. That scent had aroused in him a need to be needed, and it was happening again. This time though, it brought with it an awareness of his second mind, his second sight, and his sixth sense.

He remembered his mother telling him how to listen to the things that were around and inside him. Whenever he listened closely, he could hear his own heartbeat. Closer still and he could hear the heartbeat of others. Within those beats, he heard thoughts and desires, dreams and nightmares. Ross had long ago learned how to shut these things out. The hearing had always been too much, a burden he didn't want to bear. Sometimes when he felt the need, he opened up to the vibrations and the voices. This time, however, he had not called on the gift. It had simply come to him.

By the time Fina had returned with the coffee, Ross was thinking about destiny and free will. Most people thought that the two concepts were opposites when in fact they were connected.

"Twenty dollars for your thoughts," Fina said.

"I thought it was just a penny," Ross replied.

She smiled. "Well, you know, inflation."

Ross smiled, too, and said, "Just when you have everything laid out and you're moving in the right direction, suddenly, life takes you another way."

"Oh, yeah," Fina replied. "That's destiny. Destiny is what we think of as life, while life is the process of destiny."

Ross raised an eyebrow, and said, "Wow, she's beautiful *and* deep. Fina, do fries come with that shake?"

Ross thought for a moment that he saw Fina blush, but she quickly regained her composure.

"I've been thinking about that lately myself," Fina told him. "For a long time, I thought that I had been planning for life. Then one day I realized that I had been living for my plans. I looked around my home at all of the things that I had collected."

Fina moved toward the statue that Ross had noticed earlier.

"Take this for instance," she said. "I bought this four years ago on my first trip to South Africa." I wanted it when I first laid eyes on it, but the man who eventually sold it to me said that it was not for sale.

"He said that it had been carved by his favorite uncle, who had been imprisoned for fighting apartheid. The statue was carved during the fifteen years that he had been imprisoned. Though he didn't have the right tools, he somehow had created this beautiful piece, while held captive in ugliness.

"Well, by the time I heard the entire story," Fina continued, "I knew that I could not leave the country without the statue. It was the same feeling I had today when I saw the book. I talked and talked and finally came up with a dollar amount for the sculpture that the man could not refuse. It was enough to support his entire family for a whole month. I was so proud of myself for making that purchase. I had a piece of art that reflected an important struggle, and I had supported an entire household."

As Fina spoke, she moved toward the closet door and opened it. She pulled out another statue identical to the one in the living room.

"I bought this one at Kennedy Airport after I landed."

Ross laughed out loud. "I guess the uncle had a twin, huh?"

Fina laughed, too. To Ross, her laughter wasn't just pretty, it was music.

"The point I'm trying to make," Fina continued, "is that all of the things that I've collected throughout my life are not my life. They have no value, but what I've ascribed to them. I wanted to believe that I had a piece of the South African struggle, and that's what the man sold me."

"When we are open to face the true value of an object or person, we can sometimes be disappointed," Ross interjected.

"But why?" Fina asked. "An object is what it is, and it serves the purpose it was designed for, but only if we let it. We make the choice to see or not see its truth.

"This room is full of the memories that I have collected, but they are not my life, and they are not the journey. They simply mark the journey. When we make the choice to live within the purpose that we were designed for, we collect fewer things, but we admire many more."

Ross stood up as if to protest.

"Whoa, hold it right there," he said. "I hope that you are

not talking about love, too. I mean, how many others are you admiring?"

Fina ignored Ross's use of the word "others."

She said, "Well I wasn't thinking about love, but that's a great example. The more focused we are on our purpose, the fewer lovers you need. You can admire many people, but you don't have to own them."

The conversation went on like this for some time before Ross realized that he was inside of his own dream. He knew he was dreaming because the beautiful room he had been in before was now in black and white.

Years before, Ross had been married, and on the night before his wedding, he'd had a dream about the woman he was about to marry. This dream was in black and white, except for the vivid red apple that his now ex-wife was trying to get him to eat.

His mother had actually yelled at him for not telling her the dream earlier. This dream that he now found himself in was much more pleasant, even though it was still black and white. In this dream Fina sat across from him with her hands folded in her lap. He asked her if he could touch them when Miss Cozy appeared. She was stirring something in a pot. She looked at him and said, "Not yet. Y'all got work to do. Remember the ingredients, you have to get all of them." Ross looked back to Fina and saw that she was fading. Only her hands remained. Ross thought he must have blinked, because as soon as he did, Fina was gone and someone else appeared. Sitting in front of him now was a very dark well-dressed man. He appeared to be African, but he spoke with a Southern drawl.

"We need y'all" was all he said. And then Ross woke up. He was surprised to find himself lying on Fina's large, comfortable sofa. Sometime earlier she had covered him with a colorful patchwork quilt. He ran his hands over the surface and discovered from the varying fabric textures that some patches seemed to be much older than others. He'd seen this kind of quilt work before and knew that it was worth lots of money. Ross was touched by the fact that Fina had found him worthy of such a valuable thing. It was this thought that led him back to sleep.

When he saw the quilt again, he could hear the birds outside of Fina's window.

16.

Biscuits and Honey

When Fina rose, she felt as if she hadn't slept at all. Something was different about her apartment. As soon as she tried to see the difference, she knew the difference wasn't in something she could see. It was something she smelled. Something was baking, and the aroma was making her hungry. Thinking that the smell must be coming from her next-door neighbor, Fina closed her window. But the smell was coming from her own kitchen. She hurriedly bathed and dressed and went out to find Ross pulling a batch of biscuits out of the oven.

"Hope you're a biscuit eater," he said, smiling.

"Good morning to you, too, brotherman," Fina said. "I must have died and gone to heaven."

"I just wanted to thank you for the coffee, the conversation, and the covers," Ross told her.

Fina felt like a schoolgirl and tried not to show it.

"Just a little something I do for all of the strangers I meet in bookstores," she said sarcastically.

"Yeah, this was kind of forward of us, wasn't it?" Ross added.

"My daddy woulda tore me up," Fina said. "It was late. My daddy used to say if me or my brothers came home late: 'After eleven o'clock, ain't nothing open but your legs.'"

Ross laughed and said that their parents must have gone to the same school.

"So I guess there's nobody serious in your life," Ross said, changing the subject.

"Just my gunrunning husband with the black belt, who's off on a wild game safari," Fina said.

Ross laughed and said, "I guess it is kind of stupid to ask now."

Fina smiled and went to the cabinet to get honey for the biscuits.

"You've got a real good kitchen," Ross said as she turned her back. Fina knew that Ross was talking about more than just her physical kitchen, but didn't let on.

"Thanks" was all she could manage.

They had biscuits and tea, and broke the rules of first dates by talking about old relationships. They discovered they had a lot in common and had made many of the same mistakes. Both of them had stayed in relationships that weren't working, hoping they could make things better. Fina had to laugh when Ross told her about the woman who'd called every hour on the hour and played "Thin Line Between Love and Hate." Fina had also had a few nuts in her past. Talking about old relationships had always been taboo for her. Fina didn't like to compare or be compared. She felt that each relationship should stand on its own and should have a chance devoid of past hurts. But sitting here with Ross, she didn't feel like she was comparing notes with a potential love interest, she felt like she was talking to an old friend.

After eating biscuits with everything from jelly to honey to cheese, Ross and Fina prepared themselves to spend the day together.

While Ross showered, Fina thought about trying on his shirt. She picked it up and felt the soft white linen. She took in his scent, and had a feeling that it would fit just fine. Fina stood there for a moment holding the shirt in her hands, enjoying the feeling of the smooth fabric and then realized that the water from the shower was no longer running. Not wanting to be caught, she quickly put the shirt back as she found it. Fina wasn't quick enough. Wearing pants but no shirt, Ross entered the room. His skin was the same beautiful smooth skin she dreamt about two nights before, but she could now see what was about to be revealed in her dream. It was a large scar that appeared to have been caused by a burn. Oddly, Fina found it to be beautiful and wanted to run her fingers over it. Instead, she managed "Sorry," and ran for the living room.

Ross didn't take long. He came in the living room and said that it felt like Sunday instead of Saturday.

"Yes it does," Fina said, trying to ignore the earlier encounter. "I really thought it was Sunday, because I forgot that I had taken Friday off."

Fina wished it were Sunday. She envisioned getting ready for church together, and going to family get-togethers later.

She also thought about reading the Sunday paper together in bed. She could almost hear the delicious sounds of the paper crumpling beneath their bodies. The thought was too wonderful to contemplate, so she willed herself back to the here and now.

Ross and Fina made their way back to Miss Cozy's. It was just ten o'clock in the morning, but it felt like midnight. Much had happened in a short amount of time.

Fina got up the nerve to ask Ross about the beautiful scar. "That's my reminder," Ross said.

"Reminder of what?" Fina wanted to know.

Ross told her about his early childhood. Fina was silent the entire way. She remembered what her father told her about being a good listener. When Ross was through with tears in her eyes Fina said, "Looks like you could use a good friend."

Ross squeezed her hand and said, "Look who's talking, ice queen."

They laughed and actually ran the last block to Black Images.

When Ross and Fina reached Black Images, Miss Cozy was already running for the door. They could see that she was excited. She flung the door open wider and did a crazy little dance. "Hey now, hey now," she said, clapping her hands as she did the old folks' shuffle. Miss Cozy was holding *Children of*

Grace and another book. She held it up for Ross and Fina to see. "Look familiar?" she said to Ross. She was holding a copy of Ross's dissertation. "I had this sent over from the university press. Boy you're a scholar's scholar," she said excitedly. "Your chapter on *Children of Grace* is good, real good. It's amazing what you were able to piece together without ever seeing the book."

Ross blushed and said, "Thanks. You can imagine the trouble I had trying to write about black folklore for a committee of people who didn't even understand black reality."

Fina grabbed the book and found the table of contents. Without saying anything to Ross or Miss Cozy, she spotted a corner and walked toward it. She wanted to find out why Miss Cozy was so excited.

"Get back over here," Miss Cozy said to Fina. "Girl, we got work to do. This boy knows a lot, but he doesn't know everything. And I suspect that you know more than you've been telling. But before we get to all that," Miss Cozy continued, "I need to tell you all something I think you'll want to know."

Miss Cozy ushered them back to the patio. Snacks and beverages had already been set up. "Sit down, sit down," Miss Cozy said.

She took a hard look back at Ross and then she looked at Fina. "Well, I see that one of us has on the same clothes he had on yesterday, so I can tell who went to whose house."

Fina blushed and became defensive. "No ma'am," she said loudly, "it wasn't what you're thinking."

"Look here, Miss Too," Miss Cozy exclaimed, "you don't know *what* I'm thinking. I was just making an observation. Don't get all high and mighty with me."

Fina had been checked twice this morning and she wasn't accustomed to it. She almost cried but then she felt stupid that she was even bothered by what was just Miss Cozy's way. Fina checked her ego and said, "I'm sorry, Miss Cozy,"

Miss Cozy said, "You can apologize, but don't ever be sorry."

Now Fina laughed. Then she smiled and said, "My father always said the same thing."

"Well, I see you didn't listen to him either," Miss Cozy

said, smiling. "Now, where was I before this brother's clothes interrupted? Oh yes." She was remembering. "I want to tell you both something you need to know."

"This book," she said, holding up *Children of Grace*, "is more than Iona's story. There is a secret to it." Then Miss Cozy paused and stared at the two of them.

"Okay," Ross said. "Are we going to find out or not?"

Miss Cozy said, "Now, why do you think you're here? I don't feed all of my customers, you know."

Fina, not wanting any more correction, sat quietly.

"I think we should pray," Miss Cozy said suddenly. "Dear Lord," she began, "we thank you for the task you have set before us. Make us worthy, responsible, and humble. Amen."

Ross wanted to say something about the brevity of the prayer, but he thought it better not to.

"Amen," Fina said. "Thank you, Miss Cozy. Now I'm dying to hear about the book."

"Watch your words, chile," Miss Cozy told her. "You ain't going nowhere yet.

"Well, as I said, this book is more than just a story. True, the story is both beautiful and painful, but it also holds principles that can help us see our way around life's problems."

Ross and Fina looked at each other and then back at Miss Cozy. "You mean like *The Celestine Prophecy*?" Fina asked.

"Sort of," Miss Cozy said. "But I believe it's something more. This message comes from our ancestors—our black mothers and fathers who shaped a life for us long ago. These principles are called the 'Recipe of Life.'

"Ross Buchanan," Miss Cozy said, "you stumbled all over it in your dissertation, but there was no way you'd have found out without the actual book. Before I continue, tell me why it is you never came here for *Children of Grace*. You've been here at least three times over the past four years. You should have figured out that I'd at least know something."

Ross made a face and bowed his head, "Yes ma'am. I should have," he said. "But my arrogance didn't allow me to look in the obvious place."

"Uh-huh," Miss Cozy said. "What would an old black woman ever know about the past? Right?"

Ross confessed, "I've searched every major library in the

country only to be told that nothing like this existed. And here you are with the book and all this information. I feel like a fool," Ross admitted.

"Well, chile, we all act foolish sometimes. Trick is to not stay that way. Besides, you may as well prepare yourselves. I have the feeling that before we're done we all gonna feel foolish.

"Anyway," she continued, "the Recipe of Life is the principles of truth contained in this book. Supposedly, when placed in the right hands, barriers that have held people back can be removed. The barriers are spiritual and so is our battle. We've been under spiritual warfare."

Ross felt dizzy. Miss Cozy's revelation was mind-boggling.

Fina was so excited to be a part of all this. She said, "What if I hadn't taken off work for a day? I wouldn't be here. What a coincidence!" she said.

Miss Cozy just laughed. "Chile, there are no coincidences. Now," she said to Fina, "it's time to tell us what you know."

17.

More Pages, More Truth

🌿 Fina sat motionless for some time. No one said anything. Miss Cozy felt it was important to allow this child to tell things in her own way. She was accustomed to having the gift of "second sight," as her mother called it. But there were some things she didn't know. This was one of those times when she had to rely on someone else's gift.

Fina sat up and readied herself. She cleared her throat, knowing that she didn't need to, but felt like doing it. In a way, it cleared her path to speak. "I told you that it was my father who told me about this book," she reminded. "Well, he told me something else about it. There's more to the book," she said. "I know the story, but not all of it. And neither do you, Miss Cozy. There are more pages, more truth."

Miss Cozy stood up and wanted to say something, but she

caught herself and sat back down. "Go on, chile, don't let my foolishness stop you."

"There's supposed to be some power attached to the book," Fina continued. "They say that the one who possesses it also possesses the gift of knowing. It's some ability to see into the lives of others. . . . Before I go on, I need to know if that's true."

She looked to Miss Cozy, waiting to hear what she already felt. Just being in the presence of the book had given her clarity. She could only imagine what it was doing for Miss Cozy.

"That's right, chile," Miss Cozy said. "But I guess I didn't figure on it like that. I thought that by reading it, I was able to tap into a gift that I already had. I always thought that this book was like a switch that helped me to turn on that gift. I never knew that the book was the gift itself. There's something else you're not telling," she said to Fina.

"Yes, there is," Fina admitted. "My daddy said that it had been passed down through our family, but when my great-great-uncle was about to sell the book away, his wife removed part of it. The last section, to be exact. She knew what it meant, even though she didn't believe it. The book supposedly told of the future for blacks in this country. The story goes that a great shift in the balance of power was coming and this book had something to do with it."

Miss Cozy couldn't believe what she was hearing.

"Like I said before," Fina continued, "I just thought my daddy was making up stories to entertain me. If I had known the book really existed, I would've beat Ross in here by about ten years."

"Well, what are we waiting for? Didn't you see *Raiders of the Lost Ark*? Come on, why should white folks be the only ones with some adventure?" Ross said.

Miss Cozy looked at him through one eye. Ross had seen this look before. "Boy, do you know what's she's saying? This ain't no game; no treasure hunt to make you famous. This is about destiny. You standing there grinning like you trying to win the lottery or something. I suggest you be real prayerful and stay focused."

Ross apologized and thought about his reaction. He couldn't help it, though. He felt like he was still a kid reading a mystery novel. Only this time, everything in it was real. So real that his body reacted to it.

Fina said, "He's right, though. We should be reading and trying to put things together. I mean, our people are not doing any better than they were twenty years ago."

"Some are, most aren't," Miss Cozy added. "There seemed to be something happening in the twenties with the Harlem Renaissance and all. Then I thought for sure we were getting there in the sixties, but then folks started fighting each other. Those who weren't killed off were bought out."

"I hear you loud and clear," Ross said. "Would have been something to see black folks move on in the way they had been moving."

"Yeah, but give a black man a Brooks Brothers suit and a white woman and he will sell his mama," Fina commented angrily.

"Alright, Ms. Ndegeocello!" Ross said, referring to the singer Fina had quoted.

"When y'all are through being in love, I'll be ready to read."

Ross and Fina tried to ignore Miss Cozy's remark, but had

to smile. They walked out to the back patio and sat in the same seats as the day before.

"Who wants to read?" Miss Cozy asked.

"I will," Fina said. She reached for the sacred book, realizing how precious it was, and she began to read.

18.

Knowing What Love Is

🌱 What I'm writing is true. But just because it's true don't mean it's right. I did go wash. I try to wash away all that boy leave inside me and on me. I try to wash away what I know about my mama, and what I don't know. And I try to wash away what happen to Miss Miella and what happen to me. But the more I wash, the dirtier I feel. It was almost night time when my daddy come find me. They say I was half drown.

I didn't speak on what happen but everybody know.

Wasn't nothing that hadn't been happening. The older women come around me and whisper love in my ears. The men just stay away, even my daddy. I don't want him to see me no way. I was shame for myself. All the washing in the world ain't make me clean.

Some folks say I take it too hard. They say I was spoilt and need to learn what I was for anyhow. I don't see it that way. Just cause folks get used to pain don't mean they should keep specting it.

Wasn't nothing nobody say that make me better. I was still afraid to be better. Seem like better days brought on worse. My time was past and I had to get back to my work. My daddy keep me closer still. That's when I see Joe again.

He come round real quiet at first. He wouldn't say nothing to me, he just sit there like he waiting for me to talk. He would hold his head low, like doing that made me not see him. Time go by, but we still slaves.

One day, my daddy leave me and Joe again. That's when Joe talk to me. He tell me that he sorry for all that happen and that he wish he can change it. He want to kill that boy, but my daddy talk some sense into him.

Daddy say, "Then who she gonna have to love?"

That almost make me smile, and I tell him so. Joe hold me close then like I ain't never been held. I can still smell his skin. Sweet like cane, but salty, too. He's smooth all over cept for his back. He had scars from beatins, lots of em. He tell me it from when he try to run away before he come to live here.

I tell him his back look like it got trails all over it.

He smile and tell me those was the roads to freedom. Cept them roads ain't go nowhere.

It was only when he stop running that he get to come here with me.

He say I his freedom. Cause when he think of me, he free in his head.

Then Joe kiss me like before, but this time he touch me, too. Then he hold me like a man hold a woman when he love her.

Now I'm a tell you true, ain't nothing can bring back your life when it taken away, but Joe do something else. He make me know that I'm still myself. That was the last time my daddy sleep in the same place as me.

From then on me and Joe was married. We ain't never have no kind of celebration or nothing. We just move on like we was sposed to. Folks got to whispering bout how this time my pain brought me joy and I guess they was right.

But, I know not to be happy too quick.

My belly start getting real big. I know from watching the moon that it be too soon to be Joe's baby and I turn back inside myself.

That baby came here looking like every other child that Hunn boy had. I was sad, but seem like Joe want to die. I don't know nothing bout what men really feel, and they don't tell you, but I figure that something was took from him, too. That piece I do know.

I love my chile anyway, so that's what I name him. I call him Mine. Folks say that ain't no kinda name, but I don't care. I want to have my own family, but this is what I got. Joe turn quiet even toward me, and my daddy wasn't saying much either. They both know I ain't done nothing wrong, but they feel shame for me and they feel bad that they can't even protect me.

That baby boy was growing good, and that Hunn boy keep coming round. I don't think he even look at that chile of his too good.

One day he say to Joe, "That's a real cute thing you got."

Joe ain't say nothing, cause he know he can't. But I was glad for that. I can't stand to lose him.

Joe stop holding me altogether after that. He never stopped loving me, though. He tell me so. Something just won't let him be with me. Sometimes he look at me like he want to, but then he just walk off.

Our love was still deeper than anything I ever see. Joe was sweet to me. He always make me little things from wood. Sometimes he even comb my hair. He comb it til I fall asleep. Other times, he tell me stories that his mama tell him. And sometimes we just sit quiet.

Back then when I would talk to the stars, Joe would ask me to talk to them for him, too. He want me to tell them stars about him and his mama, and all that she tell him. He say then later somebody else who listen will know all about him. I tell him to talk to the stars hisself, but he say they *my* stars, and they will only listen to me.

That make me laugh. He do other real sweet things, too. Every now and agin when the Hunn men go away, Miss Hunn give everybody some time away from they chores. Not the whole day, and not all the time, but she let everybody come out the fields when it too hot, and she say Sunday was for God. She try to be decent, but whenever the men was around, she act like she been acting before, real uppity like. I guess white women have to know they place, too. Anyway, on days like that when we get time to ourself, Joe take me to a place by the river where not too many folks go to. It's on the Hunn land, so we ain't run off. He put me in that water, and wash me all over like I'm his chile. He sing songs from his home in Africa. He touch me everywhere, but he still don't hold me like before. He make me feel good, though. One a them times, Joe wash me all over, then he kiss me. He kiss me everywhere. I feel so good, like nothing bad ever happen to me. But when I try to kiss him back like he kissing me, Joe get mad. He say "Is that what you do with that Hunn boy?" He walk off and leave me. But I catch up to him and he crying. Wasn't nothing for us to say, so we didn't. Later that night, Joe say he love me more than anything and he sorry for getting mad at me. He say he ain't never mad at me, but he can't do nothing to protect me. And he can't do nothing to the ones he really mad at. He say if he do, I'm a be the one to pay. He cry again, and this time I sing to him. We fall asleep knowing what love is.

That Hunn boy can't stand to see Joe look at me. It make him real crazy. Here we trapped in they madness, and they hating us because of it.

Even though he was doing what Joe can't, he want more. That boy want me to love him. He ask why I don't look at him like I look at Joe.

I must have lost my mind when he ask me that cause I went to laughing in his face. I couldn't stop. I just laugh at him. He drag me to the fields and do what he always do, and then he beat me bad. He tell me that I ain't nothing and neither was my mama, or Miss Miella. He beat me til all I can see is my own blood. I don't holler, though, cause I can't. My ears are full of blood and my mouth is in pieces. But I guess I don't look bad enough for him, cause he beat me some more. Then, he kick me hard, and he say, "You ain't never gonna have no more babies by nobody."

Now I understand why scars on the outside heal faster than the ones on the inside.

I crawl back to my place cause I still have a chile to live for. True, that chile was half Hunn, but I think if I live, it be more of mine.

Joe and my daddy see me at the same time and my daddy, the man who raise me, lost his mind.

All the times he wanted to protect me and can't, must have come to him. I know it wasn't because he see me as his property, but cause he love me. My daddy, who been a quiet man, who always do what he was told, take one look at me and do the last thing anybody ever spected from him.

He went and grab something from the barn, something sharp. He run and kill the first thing he see.

It was old man Hunn.

Man must not know what hit him. My daddy was gone crazy. I don't want to say what happen to my daddy, cause I can't stand to think about it. They kill him, but before they do, they do stuff. I just can't talk about. Then they shoot him down like a rabid dog.

That's how they look at it, too. Say my daddy been a good slave and that something he ate must've made him crazy.

That Hunn boy act like that's all that happened.

Right after that, he say Joe has to go. He sell my man and my chile on the same day that we bury my daddy.

redemption song

Before Joe leave, he tell me that he coming back for me. Then he take his only shirt off and give it to me. I hold on to his shirt. And I wear it every day right under my own dress. I don't care how hot it get. I got Joe's sugar salt smell right next to me and I like the way it fit. I know if I keep wearing it, he gonna come back for me.

19.
Unfilled Love

🕯 Fina couldn't speak. She knew that she wasn't the only woman to wear a man's shirt, but hearing how Iona had also worn Joe's shirt gave her all the comfort she needed.

Although the story was heavy on her heart, she also felt some peace.

This time it was Ross who wept. But, unlike Fina, he cried out aloud. It started as a sob and developed into a gut-wrenching wail. He thought of what had happened to Iona and wanted to hurt someone.

Miss Cozy sat in silence and watched as Fina and Ross, a couple who'd been united by an old book, reacted viscerally to events that happened more than a century ago.

Cozy's grandmother had told her that the book was not for everyone, but she had hoped to find someone special to experience it with. She had never allowed the men in her life to read the book. Most men were already intimidated by her anyway, and even those who didn't want to admit it were secretly jealous of the time she spent with her books. Cozy was a true book lover through and through: She slept, breathed, talked, and walked books, and a lot of men simply couldn't cope. "Woman, why you always talkin' this foolishness? Talkin' about books like they yo babies! Ain't I yo baby?" one suitor had asked her.

She believed that there were potential beaux out there who would understand the power of *Children of Grace*; she just hadn't met them yet.

As Ross continued to cry, Miss Cozy wondered how many men would have the courage to respond to the book like Ross. Ross had allowed the words to seep inside him. Miss Cozy wished she could find a man filled with so much passion.

Her loves had often been scholars, lecturers, or writers she'd met back when she first opened her store. Miss Cozy was attracted to powerful, spiritual men, but none seemed to use their power in the right way. These men spoke powerful words, but somehow they never applied the truth in their own lives. The people they taught or spoke to, or the ones who read their books would not have believed the kind of men they were in real life. The Scriptures say these are men who had a form of godliness, but they deny the power thereof.

Miss Cozy looked at Ross and thought about how different he was from the men she knew, and she was happy for Fina. Fina would have the kind of love that Iona talked about, that love that lets you be you. Miss Cozy was still smiling and Fina was wondering how Miss Cozy could look so happy while Ross was in so much pain.

Miss Cozy motioned for Fina to come inside with her.

"It's time for us to eat something," she said.

Fina took the old woman's hint and followed her inside.

20.
Chasing the Blues Away

Soon wonderful smells filled the air and Fina was beginning to feel better.

"Nothing like a good homemade meal to take the blues away," Miss Cozy said.

"I thought that was good loving," Fina said.

"Good loving, good meal—same thing." Miss Cozy and Fina both laughed. Fina became more comfortable with Miss Cozy's way and realized that she needed the company of older women.

They began to talk like old friends do when they haven't seen one another for a long time but pick up right where they left off. Miss Cozy shared with Fina what she had been thinking earlier as she watched Ross's reaction to the story. She told her that the men in her life had been jealous of her and her books.

"They all had been important men," she said, "and they couldn't understand how I could let my work, my purpose, be more important than taking care of them."

"Men are like that," Fina added. "They want a woman who's together and then the very thing that attracts them is the thing that ultimately drives them away."

A silence fell over them as Fina checked her watch. She had heard somewhere that there was always a lull in the conversation at twenty minutes after or twenty minutes before the hour. Now, whenever she was engaged in conversation and the silence fell, she checked her watch out of curiosity. Sure enough, it was twenty past the hour, and she wondered why.

"That's because everyone has an internal clock, and basically we all need breaks around the same time, all the time," Miss Cozy said.

Fina hadn't spoken a word of what she'd been thinking, and realized that Miss Cozy's gift was something she'd have to get used to.

"How did having the gift make your male friends feel?" Fina asked.

Miss Cozy laughed and said, "Chile, it's been hard to deal with. And believe me, that's an understatement.

"It's not a good thing to know more than the folks around you, and it's never a good thing to know all that they're thinking and planning to do. I've been hurt badly by it. But I still wouldn't trade this gift for anything. How can you walk away from your calling?" Miss Cozy smiled and then paused. "But let's get back to you and that fine piece of man downstairs."

Fina began to beam, and Ross walked into the room. "Something smells g-o-o-d," he said, trying hard not to show any emotion.

Fina looked up and saw the pain that Ross was in. Even though he tried to hide it, he wore it openly. She felt bad for whatever he was experiencing, but she really didn't know how to respond. Despite growing up in a house full of men, Fina had never truly seen their pain. Her brothers had either been cracking jokes or profiling; they were too cool to show any real emotions. Her father had wept when her brother died, and then again at her mother's funeral, but his was a silent sadness. He never really allowed her to feel his pain either.

Whenever Fina finally found the strength to break up with a man because the relationship was going nowhere, even the most needy brothers walked away as if their time together meant nothing.

She wondered what it was that made Ross so different. How had he managed to break down the wall between black manhood and his inner self? In her heart, Fina knew that Ross's reaction had been honest. But in her head, she prepared herself for the possibility that Ross would someday act as if he had never been that emotional.

Yeah, let me take notes, she thought to herself. *'Cause as soon as this is over, the "cool" is going to rise up like it never happened.*

Ross hadn't yet fully recovered. His eyes were swollen and his face was still somewhat ashen. He held his head down and asked Miss Cozy where the bathroom was.

"Down the hall, first door on the right."

As he walked away, Miss Cozy mouthed the word "fine," and Fina laughed out loud.

"I heard that!" Ross shot back. "You act like you ain't never seen a man cry before."

"We have," yelled Fina, "he just wasn't as fine as you."

Several minutes later Ross rejoined Fina and Miss Cozy. "I need to apologize for the way I reacted. I mean . . . I guess I needed a good cry," he added.

"We all do," Miss Cozy said. "I have one at least once a week."

"I get in a real good one once a month," Fina said. "Usually around that time. In fact, I have never broken up with anyone outside of that time of the month. It brings on truth."

Ross tried to ignore her, but he had to smile. He loved that this woman was being so honest.

"Really," Fina said, "I have to say whatever I'm thinking when I'm on my period."

"Thank you," Ross said loudly. "I get the picture."

Miss Cozy joined in. "I used to be the same way. I had to say whatever was on my mind. Ross, you need to do a study on it and check out the connection between a woman's cycle and how honest she becomes. You can look at it over time. I bet they have cave paintings and all," she teased.

"Thank you, but no, I'll stick with what I'm working on."

They laughed some more, then Fina became serious and

asked, "Ross, I want to know what made you react like that. Do you cry often?"

Ross shook his head and said, "Before today, I hadn't cried in about ten years."

"Good God, man!" Miss Cozy yelled. "It's a wonder you didn't turn into a piece of wood."

"What was it that made you cry ten years ago?" Fina asked.

Ross sat still and took a moment to compose himself. "That's when I decided to find out who my parents were. I tracked down my biological mother, but by then she had already died. Now, if you don't mind, I don't want to discuss it."

Miss Cozy put her hand on Ross's head and held it there. Tears streamed down her face and onto the top of his head. They sat in silence. Several minutes later Fina rose and prepared a large plate for Ross and said, "Here, man, chase your blues away."

21.

without a vision, people perish

As they finished the meal and cleaned the kitchen together, Miss Cozy asked Ross to explain further what he'd felt when he heard the story. "I need to know what men go through."

Ross sat down and sighed. "It was a release, I guess. I know how those men felt. We brothers don't go through what a sister goes through, and yet we do. We feel *something* because we're connected to you. It's just hard to identify it. Even today, there's little we can do to really make it better for you. Instead of trying, we turn away in our shame. Most women think we don't care. We do. We just don't know how to fix things. We end up leaving or turning on ourselves. Men leave because they can't handle what women are forced to handle. We'll tell you that we don't want the pressure, but in truth we just don't know what to do with it. All the 'good loving' seminars in the world can't teach us how to be who we really are. I realized today that something happened on those plantations that took our joy, too."

Ross paused and looked down at his hands and continued. "I guess that's a sorry excuse. But, sometimes we do feel that women won't let us be the man. That even sounds crazy to me. We have to be the man. A woman can't make us be something that she's not.

"Somewhere in our past, things have gotten real messed up and I'm just tired of running."

Fina reached out and put her hand on the top of his. She held it there and said, "Please, let me help you?"

All Ross could say was "You already have."

Miss Cozy served Ross a big piece of red-velvet cake and reveled in the comfort that she felt. It was almost as if she were spending time with her own son and daughter-in-law. There was warmth in the kitchen and no one wanted to leave. The walls smelled of vanilla, baked in over time, and Ross said so. This was where they all needed to be.

"I feel like starting something," Fina said.

"Uh-huh," Ross replied. "Y'all want to start the Let's Make All Black Men Cry club."

Fina sucked her teeth and rolled her eyes. "No," she continued. "I feel like we're learning things and feeling stories that need to be passed on."

She looked to Miss Cozy. "You mentioned earlier about the movements of the twenties and the sixties. You were right. Real progress was made. People were just beginning to tell our own stories and love ourselves. Something always came in and snatched it away."

Ross was in agreement. He added that every time blacks had gained a little ground, though, their movements had been destroyed by government infiltrators and webs of deception.

"You better be careful, Miss Cozy," he said. "This room is probably bugged."

"Don't think I haven't checked," she said. She smiled, but something in her eyes said she wasn't joking.

"You're right about the government," Miss Cozy agreed, "but we played a part in our own downfall."

"How is that?" Fina asked. "Ross is right, they harassed any black person who worked for change. Even writers and singers were on the FBI hit list. The 'Powers That Be' go to any lengths to stop us from progressing."

"True that!" Miss Cozy added, crossing her arms, imitating a homeboy. "But the truth is as the Bible put it, 'without a vision people perish.' Our problem, though, is that we have turned our back on God's vision for our lives and have taken on someone else's vision. Just think about it. Even our idea of beauty is not our own."

"Speak for yourself," Ross said. "I know what I like," he added, looking directly at Fina. "I ain't trying to find no size-two Barbie. Besides, the only thing I like flat is my pancakes."

Fina tried hard not to blush, but did so anyway. She always enjoyed being admired for how she looked. She grew up liking herself, and then like most women, allowed the media's nonsense to alter her good sense. She'd spent years trying to fit in with society's notion of beauty until one summer while home from college some brothers on the corner yelled, "Thank God for real sisters!"

From then on, she decided that she'd no longer try to fit into Calvin Klein's or any other designer's clothes that didn't fit her comfortably.

Fina began to search for black designers and anyone else who understood her proportions. She was happy to discover

Moshood, a Brooklyn-based designer whose clothes fit her tiny waist, but had room enough for her large round behind.

It took some men on the corner, who society would have labeled "worthless," to teach her again that she was beautiful. She thought of the irony in this and caught Miss Cozy's smile.

"Yes, chile, that's what I'm talking about. We have to stop accepting other people's ideas of success, or prosperity, and search for peace. Having stuff don't make you nobody. We keep thinking that if we buy more stuff we'll be better."

Ross smiled because he knew he was about to get a speech.

"Ain't no need of thinking them thoughts. Just get some more cake and listen."

Ross was happy to do as he was told.

"You remember what happened after Moses led those folks out of Egypt?" Miss Cozy asked. She didn't wait for a response, but kept going since she was on a roll. "Well, Moses went up to the mountains to talk to God. 'I'll be back,' he told them folks. Well, as soon as he was gone, those people who had seen all of those plagues and miracles went to Aaron and said, 'Make us an idol so we can worship it. This will be the god we thank for setting us free.'

"What's real crazy is that Aaron, the man who had been speaking for Moses, went right on and did it. I mean, all those frogs would have been enough for me. But those folks had to have a golden calf. Moses came back and asked Aaron what happened, and Aaron went to lying. 'Well, your people asked for a god, so I put their gold in the fire and that golden calf came out.' He never bothered to say, 'I'm the one that molded and crafted the thing.'

"What I'm saying, son, is this: Nobody can take us out unless we provide the opportunity. We're the ones who mold and craft it for them.

"What destroyed each and every slave revolt?" Before they could say, she had again answered herself.

"Some master-loving black person who couldn't wait to be the Tom. That Tom always thought that turning on his own would make him better in the eyes of white folks. We got to stand guard and be ready. Folks like Malcolm knew that. And look at Winnie Mandela. Everybody wanting to hate her for the things she was forced to do. But I don't know what any of us would have done in her situation, do you?

"What we have to do," Miss Cozy concluded, "is learn from

the mistakes of each and every movement and revolt. We have to study what went wrong and make sure it doesn't happen again. We do need a movement. We need to move back to what God has already planned. Because I read the book, and I know that we win.

"Now, before I read another thing I need to talk some more about that recipe," Miss Cozy said.

"Yes, the Recipe of Life," Fina added. "I've already learned quite a bit, but I don't know how this is going to change my life."

Miss Cozy laughed. "Well, chile, you don't understand because what you been learning ain't just about you or for you." And then she continued. "You see how Ross reacted to that book, and you remember how you felt hearing about what happened to Iona and her people, don't you?"

"Of course," Fina replied, but then corrected herself. "I mean, yes, Miss Cozy."

"Well what did Iona say about good times and bad times?"

"Iona was afraid to have good times because she was afraid that they brought on the bad times," Ross answered.

"Right," the older woman said. "Have either of you ever felt this way?"

A trigger went off in Fina's brain, and she was overwhelmed by a memory that she'd long forgotten.

Right before her mother died, Fina had been on a camping trip with her school. She was having the best day of her twelve-year-old life, when the teacher called her away from the group and told her she had to go home. The school had received a call saying that her mother had died.

Since then Fina had a fear of being happy and was only now able to understand why.

It was then that they learned the first part of the recipe.

"Black people," Miss Cozy said, "have to accept that we are entitled to be happy. Our ancestors paid the price for us through slavery, but we still don't understand that it's our right, our birthright, to be happy. We've become so accustomed to misery that we think we're supposed to be unhappy. And if there isn't any misery in our lives, we'll either find some or create some. Then we either ignore our history or become trapped in it. We have to constantly remind ourselves that we deserve joy, that we deserve peace. And we have to pass this message along to the children. That's the way the ancestors want it."

Ross looked at Fina and said, "I don't know about you, but I've got a new goal in life."

"What's that?" Fina asked.

"To be happy. You want to join me?" he asked slyly.

"Give me the pages, boy, before I smack you into the middle of next week." Miss Cozy said as she pulled back the pages and began to read. But this time they braced themselves for what the book would reveal next.

22.

WHEN LOVE COMES BACK

Telling my story is hard. But wasn't nothing harder than living it.

Before Joe was sold away, I figure out that bad stuff gonna happen no matter what I do. I even know now that I wasn't causing it to be. Still I ain't have nothing left to be joyful bout.

Sometimes I think back on that day. I be trying to figure out why it all come to be. Things were as they were, but I was wishing my daddy kill the boy instead. I guess he was trying to tear the tree down by the root. In a way, it work, too. That boy never bother me no more.

I think he was scared of what I might do. Folks see me talk to the stars and got to saying I was some kind of root worker. I was just trying to talk to Joe.

Still, that young Hunn wouldn't sell me off. I guess he feel like that might make me think I won. Whatever he thinking I don't care. I was getting ready cause I know Joe to do just what he say. He say he coming back and I know he was.

I keep going back to what Miss Miella say and trying to see my strength. My scars heal, but that boy was right. I wasn't gonna have no more babies. Don't ask me how I know. Just something inside me feel all tore up. Since all my family was gone, I got to talking to God. I didn't talk like the preachers who they lowed to come round did. I talk to God like I'm talking to you, just plain like.

I know God hear me, cause I ain't so angry no more. Talking to God change me and help to make me right for my future. Lots of folks think that when they pray, they should get they answer right away. I know by watching plants that everything has a season. Just wasn't my season yet.

I had a chile out there somewhere, and he was gonna have children. It might not be until his children's children come along, but I know my time is coming.

Life move on, time move on. Look like I'm a die the same way I live—without nothing to call my own. Then one day, about ten years later, when I'm out finding plants, I hear someone yelling my name. I don't turn cause that voice was familiar and close to my heart.

I figure it had to be in my head cause all the folks that was close to my heart was gone. I wasn't never letting nobody get next to me again.

That voice got louder and louder til I could feel the voice holding me. I just stand there cause I figure I'm either dead or crazy. When I commence to turn round I see my dream before my eyes. My Joe come back and he was right there, showing the same smile that made me love him. I cried and cried, cause some small part of me was still specting that pain that always came when I had joy.

He wern't with no white folks and he was dressed real fancy. I couldn't do nothing but cry. He say my name over and over— "Iona," "Iona," "Iona." Then, he hold up some papers and say "I own her." I can't read them, but I know what he was meaning. Those were my free papers. I'm nobody's but his.

We hold each other all night. Right there in front of God we hold each other good. He cry, too, and tell me how much I mean to him and what happen over those ten years.

Joe say he learnt writing and he write to me. But he never send those letters, though. He just write em and hope my stars be telling me what they say. One day he get real sad and throw most of em out. He keep one letter, though, and he read it to me. He was telling me how much he love me and how much I make him feel like hisself. He say in that letter that he had to find me and that's just what he did.

Joe tell me that he been sold to one place and then to another. The last place let him hire hisself out. He worked enough to pay for hisself. He wasn't fool enough to let them know what he doing, though. He do some work for a free black man and become kindly with him. That man know some of the white abolitionist folks. Joe give his money to one of them, a Mr. Sanders, and he do the buy. Then Joe say something I can hardly believe. He say there's some white folks who on our side. He say them folks is getting beat and killed right long with us. This had to be true, or my Joe wouldn't be saying it. I just ain't never see no white folks like that.

Joe tell me bout a white woman who love a black man and have a baby for him. Up North people ain't too different from the ones down here. They beat that man dead, and they even beat they own. They must have beat they kind of sense into her, cause after they let her live and her man die, she borned that baby and left him out in the fields. Some white man come by and hear it crying, and he raise it like his own.

My man tell me all kinda stuff like that. Joe sure smart. Then he say he done real well, but he know he can't really be free unless he with me. So, here he was back in hell, trying to set me free.

He say he work real hard like he still a slave cause he want me with him. Joe always been real quiet, but now he always thinking. He tell me he think about me all the time. He say our time for children gone, but he say it's lots of children that ain't got no folks. But he tell me we can raise a mess of em. That sure make me smile and think of my daddy, the man who raise me. I tell Joe what I'm thinking and he smile, too. That's when he tell me that my daddy talk about me to him. Daddy tell Joe lots of stuff that I ain't know about. My daddy was a hardworking man, he never make no trouble til the end of his life. Truth be told, he wasn't the real cause of that trouble neither. Anyway, he say that on the day that the Iunn man kill my mama she was talking in her Africa talk. She was screaming somethin in that talk. My daddy ears don't know what she saying, but his soul do. She telling him to take care of me. She say I'm a special chile and I'm gonna set us free. My daddy tell Joe I'm gonna cook the Reape of Life. That's my daddy's code for finding the road to freedom. I tell Joe he just talking crazy cause he happy to be with me. He say no, this true. My daddy told him he call me Iona cause he own me and nobody else. Joe say now he own me. I don't know what to say, so I just sit there. All this time I be thinking I'm cursed cause so much bad done happen. Now I know sometimes bad things gotta happen to get to the good. Right then I don't know what that good was, but I find out later. Joe and me talk some more and he tell me things that don't sound then, but it all for the good later.

Then he turn kinda sad and say, "Iona, I got to tell you true. I been with other women." He say it wasn't really something he want to do, but something he had to do. He made other children. But he say he wasn't real sad about it. His children may grow up to be somebody, and at least he could live through them. I wasn't upset, and I don't get no bad thoughts, but I was sad that I couldn't give him no babies.

We talk all night under the same stars that are in the sky now. I learn how he walk right up to that boy, Hunn, who wasn't hardly a boy no more and tell him he want to buy me. Hunn was laughing so hard, he fall off his chair. But, when he see all my Joe's money, he stop laughing. I guess Hunn ain't dumb as he look. He take all that money, $800 dollars, and that Hunn boy write them papers right there. Joe ask him if he has the power to do them right, and Hunn tell him he the only one who can do the papers right. Joe laugh bout how he had $2,000 dollars for me, but that man don't ask for more so he don't offer.

All this talking Joe do, but he never mention my boy. I was fraid to ask cause I don't want no pain. I had to know, so I ask. Joe say he hunt for him, but can't find him nowhere. It's almost like he disappear, Joe say. They wern't sold to the same place, but Joe felt like he shoulda found him.

My heart sink, but I can tell from talking to God and looking to the stars that my boy is alive out there in the world. There's some things you can just feel. The next day, we get ready to leave that place for good.

We shoulda left the night before.

When we get ready to go, a bunch of men with guns come standing round us. That Hunn boy say that Joe was trying to steal me away. When Joe show them the papers, they just laugh. They say wasn't nobody gonna believe no runaways. Joe try to speak truth to they might, but they beat him down. The more they beat him the more he yelled "Iona...I own her."

They laugh and beat him some more. They grab a hold of me and make me watch. I can't do nothing but talk to God. They musta thought I was working roots on them cause they take a rifle a hit me in my mouth.

When I come to, one of them is on top of me saying "Let's see what's so good that he came all this way for."

I'm gonna tell you true, cause that's the only way I know to tell it. I lay there and wish I died. I was wishing hard. I finally come to myself and I found out that I was still alive but my Joe was gone. I wonder why I been left to live. Not by those white men, I knew they didn't care nothing about me. But I wonder what else God want me to go through.

When I find that I could write then I start to see the reason. I was left here to tell this story. The whole thing. I start to see things. Things I shouldn't know, and I begin to believe that God was answering my prayers. Not for me, but for my future, my children of grace.

Miss Cozy placed the book in her lap. She began to shake and weep uncontrollably. As Ross and Fina approached her, she held up a hand and waved them away.

When Miss Cozy came around she told them that what Fina said about there being another part of the book made sense. She had always thought this to be the end of the book, and never bothered to wonder if there was more. She checked her watch and said, "Come on, we got work to do."

23.
Coming Together

🔥 Ross and Fina followed Miss Cozy down the stairs and out to the car. "Get in," she said, handing the keys to Ross. "You drive, 'cause you know the way."

Ross and Fina were puzzled, but followed the older woman's instructions and climbed into her SUV. Ross turned to Miss Cozy and said, "Okay, where to?"

"Your place," she snapped, as if he were a cabbie. Then, winking at Fina, she added, "Home, James."

"My place?" Ross asked. "What for?"

"I need to get a look at those papers you had from that class. Plus, Fina would like to see how *you* live," Miss Cozy said, laughing like an old matchmaker as Ross shook his head and started the car.

Fina hummed along to Will Downing's song, "Love's the

Place to Be" that was coming from Miss Cozy's CD player. "Gone, Miss Cozy! You down with Will?"

The older woman sucked her teeth. "Chile, who you think taught him to sing?"

Except for the music playing in the background, they rode the rest of the way in silence. Ross took Joe's death hard and had secretly hoped that Joe and Iona would live happily ever after. But he knew that black people seldom believed in fairy tales and that happily ever after only existed in Will Downing songs. Fina was thinking about the story and its connection to her life.

Miss Cozy was contemplating the mysteries that would be unlocked only after they found the rest of the book. *There's much to do,* she thought to herself.

Ross's place was a restored brownstone. It was filled with African and Native American artifacts. It reminded Fina of the black museum that her father's friend owned, which she had visited every Saturday as a child.

She loved to make up stories as she wandered through the museum. One day she found an old Indian arrowhead and decided that it belonged to a chief who had rescued a young child from white invaders. The African masks had been used in rituals that were both ancient and powerful.

Standing here in Ross's home, she recalled how vivid her imagination had once been. She wondered why she'd never explored writing. "You still got time," Miss Cozy answered, and Fina, somewhat startled, nodded her head and smiled.

Miss Cozy whispered, "Nice place. What do you do, smuggle artifacts?"

Ross laughed. "No. My biological father left me a little money along with this old brownstone. I've done a lot of work on this place, believe me."

As she stepped into the living room, Fina reached out and ran her hand lightly over the intricate wood paneling. The deep mahogany looked like it had been restored to its original condition. "Real nice work. But I thought you never knew your father."

"I didn't," Ross replied, "but he knew about me and actually had me tracked down. Seems crazy to do after you're dead, but I'm not complaining.

"Well, that's not completely true," Ross added. "At first, I was mad as hell. I didn't want anything to do with anything he had. After I thought about it, though, I realized that I deserved something, too, though I would have preferred to know him and to have had a relationship with him."

"Have you met any of his family?" Fina asked.

"There was no other family. . . . Weird, huh? He did leave a letter explaining himself, and a bunch of old papers and stuff that belonged to his people. I haven't had time to go through any of it. Besides, it hurts."

"Men are like that," Fina said. "You can have a package marked 'important' and you can wait a week before you open it."

Ross laughed. "That's true, but it's not like my father's box had anything to do with the Love Project."

"Well," Fina said, "let me remind you that you were the one who went searching all over the country for a book that was right here in your own town."

"I guess a part of me just doesn't—" Ross stopped in mid-sentence and turned to Miss Cozy. She was in her full glory, and grinning like a mad woman.

"But—how—I mean—I don't think . . ." While Ross was trying to get the right question in his mind, Miss Cozy was smiling and nodding.

"N-no, you *don't* think . . ." Fina stuttered. "His family couldn't have had the other papers. What are the odds of my family and his family having parts of the same book several generations back? Then on the same day, we both walk into the same store and we find it because you accidentally left it out?"

Miss Cozy laughed at her. "What are the odds?" she repeated. "Chile, don't you know destiny don't play the odds? Truth is always right under your nose. The adventure is in the preparation. Once you're ready for it, it presents itself."

24.

When the Past Looks Like the Future

🔥 "Now, where are the boxes?" Miss Cozy asked. "I'm going to get the rest of that book."

Ross fell down in a chair and began to cry. Fina couldn't help but laugh.

"Why are you laughing, woman?" Ross managed.

"Well, for a man who hasn't cried in ten years, you sure are making up for it all of a sudden."

Ross managed, what could pass for a smile and told her the truth of how he had refused to take anything from a dead man who hadn't bothered to locate him while he'd been shuttled from place to place. He'd been angry for some time after the lawyer had contacted him. Unable to function, he had taken a research sabbatical from his work. He'd never done this, so the time was due.

Once he'd seen the old house and fallen in love with the location, he accepted the gift more out of spite than any other reason. After working on the brownstone, he'd been able to release a great deal of his frustrations. He got some joy from seeing the work his hands had done. It never occurred to him that the real gift was in an old box that he'd considered junk.

There were times he'd almost thrown that box away, but he couldn't. His mother, who held on to very little, would regard anything from his past as important.

"You need to know your history," she always said.

He'd been a master at research, but he couldn't uncover his own story. He'd been afraid to do so.

"Well, what are we waiting for?" Fina asked. Ross got up and grabbed Fina by the hand.

"Alright, woman, I'm ready if you are."

Miss Cozy was pleasantly surprised to see that the attic had also been completely restored and housed Ross's office. There were several file cabinets and all the office equipment needed to start a revolution. She laughed to herself at the thought. She felt that somehow her life was wrapped up in the box she was searching for.

Even though *Children of Grace* was clearly for the two who'd come into her store at the same time in search of the same book, Miss Cozy had a strong feeling that she needed to find the missing pages first. As she scanned the room more intently, she saw a table that she hadn't noticed. It was close to a stained-glass window.

The window depicted a black woman with arms outstretched. Her head was bowed slightly, as if beckoning for some unseen multitude to come toward her. The full moon glowing behind her created an effect that caused the woman to glow. A box sat on the table under that light. It was surrounded by images she recognized, statuettes, and an old crucifix.

"Look'a here. This boy's done made an altar for the book and he didn't even know it." Miss Cozy moved toward the box but stopped to say a word of thanks. She was grateful to God, to be seen as worthy of this mission. "Lord, all I've tried to do is be available. Now help me to be mindful, prayerful and timely."

Miss Cozy opened the box and got an impression of Ross's father. She couldn't see him really but rather felt him. A keen

wave of restlessness washed over her. His father had been way-
ward as a boy and not much better as an adult. As she picked
through the box her hand brushed along something and
received a slight shock. She pulled out the papers and found the
likely cause of the sensation. It was a letter from the man to his
son—a letter to Ross from his father.

As much as she wanted to read it first, she allowed common courtesy to win over her curiosity but inched in a little
closer. As she peered deeper into the box she saw the ragged
pages of the book. She placed both hands into the box and gen-
tly removed them. She ran her hand across the page and started
to read. She could hardly believe her eyes. How could she have
been arrogant enough to believe that she'd had the entire book?
Ross and Fina gathered around her.

"Should we read it here?" Ross asked.

"What do you think?" Fina replied. "I mean, do you suggest
we go someplace where you can get some more cake?"

"No. I'm just saying it's a little cold up here and I haven't
finished the room, plus—"

"Stop running!" Miss Cozy said as she lifted her right hand
up, holding the missing pages of *Children of Grace* loosely with

her other hand. The older woman was so determined to make her point that as she moved her body back and forth, she lost hold of the book and it fell to the floor. The envelope from his father slipped from between the pages and slid across the floor.

Ross bent over slowly, picked it up, and turned it over and over in his hands. Ross wasn't quite sure what to do with the envelope marked "Son." He stared for a minute at the inscription and marveled at how much his father's handwriting resembled his own. Ross didn't know what to say or do.

Miss Cozy sensed what he was feeling and told him, "It's alright, son. You didn't know what was in the box. And even if you did, you deserved to have a cooling-off period before you decided to go through it."

"This is hard," Ross managed to say. He sat on the floor and began to read.

Dear Son,

This sounds crazy even to me, so before you go cussing me out for what I didn't do, remember I'm already gone, and you should never curse the dead.

I sure hate the way I had to do this. It was the only way, though. I ain't never brought nobody nothing but trouble, including your mama. She was a beautiful woman, but she was as wild as me. There was no way we could have done nothing for you. I heard that she passed on long ago. There wasn't no one in the family to raise you, and nobody knew how to find me.

I searched for you some time ago. When I found out that you had a nice woman raising you, and you were real smart, I thought it best for me to stay away. My life has been full of trouble. But it's been that way for everybody before me.

My seed was supposed to be the one that would make a difference. That is according to the book. I'm sure you don't know about it yet, so let me get things right.

There's a part of a book here that's important to you and your life. You turned out good enough to know what to do with it.

The history of the book is very complex, but it belongs to you now. My daddy got it from some crazy old white woman who could see the future. She said she'd gone through a lot to get it into the right hands. My daddy said that the woman had been some kinda spiritual woman or something. She'd

done some research on this book and discovered we were connected to it.

    *I don't know if you believe in all this stuff, but I hope you
do. My daddy was more trouble than me, and he says his daddy
was more than him. We trace back to a slave boy who was sold
away from his mama. His mama was the woman who wrote the
book. He was part white and for a while he tried to pass. I guess
he loved black women too much for that. Well, I say "love." He
wanted them, but he never treated them right.*

    *But all that's in the book. I'm just trying to give you a
sense of the family you never had. I'm also trying to tell you
that you were better off without us. I hope in your life you find
the peace that I never had.*

    Get some love, son. Get some peace.

Love,

Your Daddy

    Ross sat dumbfounded and couldn't speak. Much of what he
wanted to know still went unanswered. Remnants of the anger
that he'd felt for his blood father were draining out of him. Fina
looked over at him and said, "Are you alright?"

"Yes, and I only thank God that you two were here to help me bear this," Ross replied.

Without saying a word, each held this new section of the book for a few seconds and then passed it along. It ended in Miss Cozy's hands. They all sat down, and she began to read.

25.

Road to Love

The first time I see my future, I don't know what it is. It's after all that I love was killed and gone. I'm back to picking plants. I figure there was some reason to be here, so I put my life to use. I help every baby get borned and help the mothers to stay healthy.

Word got out bout what I can do and I get to go to other farms. Folks call me to fix broken bones and most everything else. I work on everybody, black and white. It's when I'm up at the Jackson place that I start seeing things.

One day I'm pulling plants for the missus over there. She say she ain't want no babies for a while, and I know just what to do. The sun was real high. I look up at it to see just how hot it was gone get. When I look down, I see bodies lying all around me. Dead men in uniforms was everywhere. Then I hear someone yelling, "The war is over! The war is over!" Later on somebody come down the road and say, "Slavery over, too!" I get so happy, I want to dance. But when I turn round my vision is gone.

When I get back to this place, I try to think on what happened. It come to me that I can't be seeing something from the past, I must be seeing into the future. I want to tell somebody, but the things I see might scare them. Sides, I don't want the white folks to know, so I just go back to work.

I long ago take over most of the cooking, so I finish up the meal. On my way out, I see the box of paper and things that the Hunn use to write with. Something in me tell me to take it, and I do. I trust my own mind because it hardly ever tell me wrong. I bring it back and just look at it for a while. Then I pick it up like I used to see that boy do when we was kids. Ain't nothing I can tell you but the truth. I commence to writing like I been doing it my whole life. The words come out of me like that preacher who be reading the Bible. I just write.

Believe me when I tell you I love the look on the faces of folks I make better. But writing make me want to sing like I did when I was a girl.

Someday I'm gonna be free. And I will be. Not me, no, but my chile's children. I start to see it all now. Look like the more I write, the more I see. I don't tell a soul, but I still tell God bout it. But God already know, cause who else can make something like this happen? I see what Joe mean, that I'm special, and that I'm gonna set us free.

I done tell you bout how I come to love Joe and all that happen to him. I tell you bout my people, they lives and they death, and how I come to be able to write. Now is time to tell you bout yourself. You my children of grace.

I see all that happen after we supposed to be free. At first things was real good. Folks went right off to look for family. Some of em find em, too. Those some happy folks. They laugh til they cry. Looking's hard work but sometimes people go into a place and name a brother or sister they ain't never laid eyes on, only to find out the person was right in front of em.

It's good to see black folk taking care of each other, too. Lot of them little ones who didn't have no family at all went right along with them folks they been used to. Not one's left behind. Everybody understand that all these children's they children, too.

Sometimes, I try to see certain things. Like I look for Joe's children. I find them, too. They grow up to be doctors and important people. He have a mess of family on down the road. He be happy to know that. When he leave this earth, he wasn't finished. We wasn't finished. He say that unless he his love with him, he's not free. I know how he feel. What ain't done in this time have to be done in the next.

The preacher say the sins of the fathers are passed on to the son. I know that just looking at that Hunn boy and his own children. But I got to believe that the goodness is pass down, too. That's when I come to know why I'm still here and why I can see so much. I gotta pass this on so that down the road me and my Joe can be free. So someone from his seed and mine can come together and finish our love.

I tell you the more I write the more I see. But I don't always like it. Seem like freedom turn into troubles for us. Folks with hoods riding horses hanging and killing as many folks as they do now. The things I write be read, and they be lost again. I'm not worried, cause I see you finding them again.

On down the road, black folks turn on each other. They fight over the best way to be free. They don't see that *the fighting* don't bring them no closer.

The words I write find they way to Joe's people. He got a beautiful family. One of them marry a man who don't believe in the power of this story. He try to win money and lose the book. His wife is smart though. She keep some so she don't lose all of this truth.

❧

Miss Cozy stopped reading and looked up at Fina. The book had in fact been in her family. The more difficult truth, however, was the fact that she, Josephine, was a direct descendant of the man Iona had loved. She was a part of this story. Her father's ramblings had been true, and the reason she'd never felt complete was that her completion was connected to this book and to this man. It was larger than the love she had looked for. It was more than the love that's represented in soap operas and romance novels. Her love and the love her people needed were connected to a revolution that was already happening. It crossed generations and found its way to her. But this was not about her. It was about generations of people who needed to be set free. She and Ross were simply a part of a larger picture.

Fina thought back to the conversation she and Ross had had the night before. They had talked about love being the only thing that conquers everything. Fina closed her eyes and held herself. In her mind she saw generations of souls trying to find their way to freedom. She was comforted by their presence. Fina opened her eyes and smiled at Miss Cozy.

This time, Fina read Miss Cozy's thoughts. "Yes," she said, "let's continue." With tears in her eyes, Miss Cozy continued to read.

Joe's children are real strong family people. They also love God. I see them tell the story even when they lose the other half of the book.

One of them children take the other half to show how important he is. He show it to some white folks who say it belong in some-place special. He act like he don't even care, just proud to be known to other people.

You gotta believe me when I say this, all white people ain't bad and all black folks ain't good. One of them white folks that work in a place of books take the time to read it cause nobody else do. Her name is Victoria, she sees that my words don't belong there, so she sneak it out. She take it to a spiritual woman who say she knows what to do.

She did what Joe couldn't do. She find my boy. Well, not him, but his seed. They all messed up on account of my baby not knowing nothing about hisself. The folks who bought him call him

James. He work in they house and play with they children on account a he so white looking. He try to be white but got tired of trying. When he get older, he look like his own people too much. But he treat the women bad. Go from one to the next and act like he a slave owner. He was still on a plantation with everybody else, but he acting like he better on account of he got some white in him. More white than black, but black runs deep, and he should know better.

I wish I had him longer. Maybe he woulda turned out better. That stuff in him passed down to his seed. None of my children's children seem to get it right. One of them almost did, but he can't hold it together. But then he have a boy that left his woman and baby.

Here I am, torn apart cause my family are taken away. It's against my will and I can't do nothing bout it. But Joe's son supposed to be free and he leave them just cause he can.

That boy he had grow up good, though. Got another mama, just like I got another daddy. The woman raise him real right. He smart, too. All that bad that was in him get chase away on account of the love that woman give him.

❧

Miss Cozy stopped reading and looked up to read Ross's face. He was smiling and shaking his head. "Unbelievable," he mumbled.

They all sat in silence. Folks had been saying the same thing for decades, but they could appreciate how important it was.

Fina said, "This makes so much sense. We always think of reincarnation as coming back as somebody else, but maybe it's about the unfulfilled longings of our ancestors."

"So true," Miss Cozy said. "That's why folks always say, 'That baby's been here before.'"

Ross thought of the folks who lost their way. "There's so much to do," he said.

"Yes," Miss Cozy said quietly. Then she went back to reading.

I'm thanking God for this gift of reading and writing cause I don't know how I come by it or why. I do know this, the one who finds the first half of this book is gonna bring our families together. They gonna have the gift of seeing just like I do. She gonna be the one to lead them to the light.

My children, you gonna have to start this family over again. It's on you to do all that Joe and me couldn't. You gotta pass on truth. You have to tell our people that they got things wrong. They done traded one slavery for another and turned their back on God. You ain't free to do what you want, you free to do what you sposed to. You have to find out what you here for, what God sent you to do. Take care of the children. Just cause they don't come from you don't mean they don't belong to you. Come back to the truth. Tell the others that they can't hate they master and want to be like him. Tell them all they did when they were slaves. How they work together and take care of one another. Tell them all they do with nothing, and how they make everything work for somebody else. They can learn they history. Tell them to love, to forgive, to never forget.

They have to stand ground cause bigger change than they seen is coming. You the beginning of that change, but be careful. Change never come without a fight. And you should know by reading this that joy never come without pain.

In your lifetime you will see a big struggle, but you have each other to get through it.

Don't let the little things keep you from doing the big things. Others will try to stop you, but things are already moving, they can't be stopped. Everybody who looks like you is not on your side. And everybody who don't is not against you.

Talk to God and never stop loving.

The more I write the more I know everything gonna be okay. I can feel it. I'm leaving these papers right here cause I know they gonna find you.

It's my time now I see that, too. Learn from this past that's yours. Take the gift of what I done seen and use it to love. This is the Recipe of Life, the road to freedom. Freedom just ain't about living free its about being free. The chains on our wrist ain't as strong as the ones on our mind. The only think that can win over evil is love. Learn to love, strive to love, cause we ain't got time for nothing else.

Miss Cozy put the book back where it had been. Ross and Fina were holding each other and crying. This time, Miss Cozy cried. She joined them and sat for a moment.

Then Miss Cozy put the book on the table where it had been. Ross and Fina were holding each other.

"Alright children, let's pray," Miss Cozy said. Ross and Fina joined hands with her and stood in a circle near what Miss Cozy had called Ross's altar.

"Dear God," Miss Cozy said, "we thank you for the opportunity to do your will. Now show us the way." Miss Cozy squeezed Fina's hand lightly and Fina took up the prayer.

"God," Fina spoke, "we are so honored to have been chosen. Teach us how to love."

Then Ross prayed. "God, this is wonderful. Show us how to stay on the right path. Keep us humble and give us the strength we need. Amen."

Ross, Fina, and Miss Cozy stood in silence for several minutes, then the older woman whispered a throaty "Amen, amen."

Miss Cozy lifted her head, opened her eyes and said, "Okay, let's figure this out."

They all sat down; Ross and Fina on the sofa, and Miss Cozy on a nearby chair. "It's time to review the Recipe.

"First, you all need to understand that too many cooks in the kitchen can ruin a meal. That's why this book wasn't out there for just anybody to find. It had to be put out there in the right time and the right way. We talked about the first ingredient."

"Right," Ross interjected. "Our entitlement to happiness and peace."

"That's right," Miss Cozy told him. "The rest are there hidden in plain view, but I couldn't find most of them cause they were in the second half.

"But here's how I figure," Miss Cozy said. "A key ingredient in the Recipe is taking care of the children who don't have anybody to take care of them. This used to be something black people just did. Folks always took in stray kids and called them their own. But now we sit and talk about the children like they don't belong to us. We have to look out for them cause we don't know what they been put here to do. We need them as much as they need us."

Ross smiled and said, "So true."

"For African Americans, family usually included people who were not blood relatives. Black folks had always taken care of other people's children," Miss Cozy said. "It was only recently, within the last twenty years, that black folks had bought into the 'I've got mine, you've got yours to get' syndrome. Before then, we raised each other's children as if they were our own. It was even common to see people raise the children of those who had caused them harm." Miss Cozy told them about a slave revolt that would have been successful had it not been for a man named Ben, who was loyal to the plantation owner. When he heard whispers of an uprising, Ben ran to his master and told him everything.

The slave owner killed all the people who had plotted against him and tortured everyone else for days. Then he did something that puzzled even white folks: He killed the woman Ben loved, and then he killed Ben.

The slave owner said that no slave could ever be trusted, especially one like Ben. "Anybody who will turn on their own is lower than a dog. Someday, that dog is gonna turn on you, too."

Ben had fathered seven children and all of them were still young, but those folks who had survived the torture took Ben's children and raised them like their own.

The ancestors knew that children belong to the entire village. This idea is as old as Africa itself. Miss Cozy said, "Until this practice is revisited, African Americans will never progress as a people.

"Alright," Miss Cozy continued. "Iona told us a lot near the end and so much along the way. She said we're not free to do what we want; we're free to do what we're supposed to do. With freedom comes responsibility and purpose. We need to be free to take care of one another, free to educate and work for ourselves, and free to find out what we're here for. Our freedom has been exchanged for materialism, and all kind of stuff that ain't got nothing to do with God's will."

Fina nodded.

"I guess you two got one of the biggest challenges though," Miss Cozy continued.

Ross and Fina were holding hands. "Ross," Miss Cozy said, "through prayer and Joe's hard labor, Iona and Joe were able to come together, but you all are gonna have to work hard to *stay* together. We spend most of the time searching for love, but once we get what we want, we stop working, but the real work still has to be done."

"Thank you, Miss Cozy," Fina said.

"Iona also told us something that I often forget," Miss Cozy continued. "She said everybody who looks like us ain't on or side, and those who don't might be. There were white folks helping us out, too. We have to be cautious of working closely with someone simply because we think they are on our side and we can't exclude folks on face alone."

"That's a hard one," Ross said.

"True, but it's a warning we have to heed," Cosina told them.

"Well, there's much for you two to do. You have been charged to set these families right. You gonna have to teach the Recipe of Life. The key ingredient is love."

Ross looked at Fina and smiled. "Learn to love, strive to love, cause we ain't got time for nothing else," Ross recited.

Fina blushed and moved in closer to Ross. Then she snapped her fingers as if remembering something. "There's more, Miss Cozy. This task is not just for us. You have to help us. You are the one to lead us to the light, the teacher Iona spoke of. A big struggle is coming and I want you there to help."

Miss Cozy blinked and tears fell down her cheeks. "Thank you, Fina. Thank you, baby." Ross bit his lower lip and thought for a moment. Then he unbuttoned his shirt and removed it. Fina saw the marks on his dark skin and thought about the scars that were on Joe's back and the backs of so many other enslaved ancestors. Fina reached over and touched Ross's scars. "These are your road to freedom."

"Yes," he whispered in her ear. Then he handed Fina his shirt. "Here, this belongs to you."

Miss Cozy breathed in, held it, and then released it, and said, "Well then, let's go."

"Go where?" Ross asked. "I'm right where I need to be," he said, holding Fina in his arms.

"You got the rest of your life to be with Fina. Right now, we got work to do."

Miss Cozy pulled the first half of the book out of the large bag she'd been carrying. "The first thing we have to do is get this thing published. Not just *Children of Grace*, the entire story, your lives included."

Acknowledgments

I began writing this book in 1995, through a series of events, including the theft of my computer and an attack of the Melissa virus; the project was at a standstill. I believe that this, too, was a necessary part of the process. Things do work together for the good of those that love God and are called according to God's purpose.

Much of what is here now could not have been completed back in 1995. Moreover, many of the folks who have been a part of this project were not in the position they needed to be in at that time. These people have kept me on track and have helped to make this project possible.

I would like to thank them.

Royal Shariyf, thank you for helping me find the book again. Your life is an inspiration.

My agent/sister/fellow abolitionist Victoria Sanders,

thank you for finding my writer's voice and making me use it. And thank you for being the spook who sat by the door.

Victoria's partner, Diane Dickensheid, thank you for putting up with my frantic calls, but most of all for putting up with Victoria. My new friend/sister warrior/editor, Janet Hill, thank you for being the kind of person who you can write something good about, without worrying that she may flip out later. You are an editor's editor. Thank you for getting in the trenches.

Roberta Spivak, Janet's assistant and cowarrior. Thanks for involving your life with the revolution. We need you.

My personal assistant and sister, Jeanine Chambers. Thanks for reading my dyslexic chicken scratch. Thanks for crying with me, praying with me and making me write. You are a person in purpose. Thanks.

The name Ross Buchanan was inspired by the lives of two men who have been my spiritual mentors: Ross Rainey, my childhood pastor who now looks down from the cloud of witnesses, thanks for teaching me to acknowledge God in all things; and Ralph Buchanan, my pastor and friend. Thanks for your revolutionary approach to ministry. It has saved my life and my work.

Fatima, Jabril, and William Berry, thanks for letting Mommy work when we were supposed to go to space camp.

Beatrice Berry, thanks for watching the kids and for teaching us the true meaning of transformation.

Winston Scully, thanks for constantly reminding me that the ancestors wanted to use me.

Thanks to the Rev. Johnny Ray Youngblood for his "Freedom Talk" and this book's hidden message: "The way out is back through."

To all the people at Doubleday in Production, Copy Editing, Managing Editorial, Subsidiary Rights, Marketing, Publicity, and Sales who worked behind the scenes. While many of you don't share my heritage, you share my passion nonethe less. Thanks so much.

To the ancestors, for letting me hear their prayers.

To the readers, for listening.

❧

By the way . . . Black Images is a *real* bookstore in Dallas, Texas, and Emma Rogers is a lot like Miss Cozy. If you know what's good for you, you'll call or stop by.